A betrayal...
A fabled symbol of power...
A long weekend...
A universe that works against you...
Too much alcohol...

A noir adventure in the bright shining sun of
Southeast Asia

While trying to recover his embezzled money,
Bert Mars stumbles upon a hunt for an artifact
that threatens revolution.

Bert is brought to the brink of ruin and
revelation in a land where loyalties are only clear
after it is too late.

The long-awaited sequel to the acclaimed *In a
Country with No Name.*

EDGE OF THE GOLDEN MOON

RON MORRIS

Villefort: New York

ISBN: paperback 978-1-939270-21-4
(ISBN: ebook 978-1-939270-19-1)

Media enquiries: 2bangkok@gmail.com; ron@nortrad.com; Jay Morris, Columbus, Indiana, USA, jayf1402@hotmail.com

First Villefort softcover edition 2026 (Ingram)

10 1 9 b 11 8 9 9 9

Cover design: Arnaud Romilly
Cover layout: Jatupol Kesornsukhon
and Ratha Titipattarananon
Author's photo: Anwar Jehsani
Photos: Ron Morris
AI is plagiarism. No AI was used in the planning, writing, editing, or graphic design of this book.

Villefort Publishing
1325 Sixth Avenue, 28th Floor
New York, New York
10019

For Kat

PROLOGUE

Hippies were in the city then—fetching braless women and shaggy-haired young men—moving through the streets, their mop-tops bobbing as they ran, some carrying expensive luggage, an anomaly anywhere else in this country. They were fleeing the revolution.

This capital city was part of the old backpacking trail, the end of the world for those seeking adventure. It was a place for tourists to skip off to another country to drink and find themselves. Adventurers, spooks, and fools all wanted that final drink in the expat bars that would soon be closed by a virtuous new regime.

The locals were watching the revolution too. The myth of their peaceful communal village life had been shattered. Old ways were abandoned as the culture became caught in the grip of far-off ideologies.

Among the locals were those few who had studied overseas in cold lonely countries and came back to live in mansions here, whiling away the slow hot days in this land-locked nation. They were the elite of this tiny Asian land, only steps ahead of the winds of change sweeping away their way of life.

Their potentate was a figurehead. Beneath his rule, the sparse population of the country had become embroiled in great power politics, as dogma and bad fortune conspired to sweep aside old reactionary ways.

From the muddy hillsides, young men were coming, brown and grim, wearing flip flops and carrying guns as they warily entered the capital, ready to take what they were owed.

Revolution, a border between one reality and the next, when every moral, boundary, and assumption that underlies life becomes uncertain.

Revolution, the child of a miscalculation of history, of a million confident wrong moves.

Into this milieu, a team of U.S. soldiers and local men, loyal to the falling regime, entered the palace. It was in the final hours before the city and nation would be lost.

The palace itself was already empty, its canaries scattered far and wide, some to be consumed by the revolutionaries, others ensconced in French splendor.

The men were looking for the artifacts of the old regime that needed safekeeping—symbols capable of rousing oppressed men to action on some day in the future.

These things lived through time, beyond the frailty of man, yet depended on the care of men and luck for their preservation.

The men who entered the palace intended to collect and preserve them for a future day when revolution might again overtake a moribund regime.

They found a royal seal and a box of inconsequential jewelry. A Buddhist image and a holy drum were deemed too old and fragile to move.

The marvelous thing that they searched for above all else was a crown, with a round, pale blue stone in its brow—a fragile diadem whose gem mirrored the moon on the nation's flag.

The moon was a prominent feature of the land, an oath in the sky that linked the physical world of unending toil to the eternity of heaven.

The crown was a thing that might, one day, decades hence, inspire love for this regime that was being overthrown today.

Yet, it could not be found.

The revolution was quickly over, and a new reality appeared. It was communism, with its privations and camps and a single party and continual assertions of progress and happiness.

Those who did not flee and who embodied the old ways eventually perished in the jungles and then in history itself, their immortal lineages shown to be fallible and weak, subsumed by the rabble they had presumed to raise themselves above.

As the nation itself was inconsequential and landlocked, neither threatening its neighbors nor wishing their overthrow, these events were quickly forgotten, thus returning the land to its sleepy state before the revolution.

You may wonder how I know about this.

This is the beginning of my own story that takes place decades after these events.

I know things—some things I do not want to know, and some things I should not let on that I know.

But I knew none of that yet.

I was busy drinking in Bangkok and fooling myself into thinking I was on top of the world.

And I wanted my money back.

1

I was summoned up to the big boss's office. It was located on the top floor of the tutoring school I taught at in Bangkok. The summons was deadly serious. I wondered what I had done wrong.

I had recently returned from an abortive attempt at a new job in a neighboring country. I had a good tale to tell, but what had happened was too strange to fully come to terms with yet. I had escaped from real danger, doing bad things in hopes of fortune and glory. I vowed I would not put myself in such danger again. I would not let my ambition get the better of me. Yet, when I escaped, I did so thinking I was smarter than everyone else. That is a fun conceit to have.

Still, I had to come crawling back to this school, begging for my old job back, and I now wondered if the big boss was having second thoughts about rehiring me.

I was back here teaching the overly attentive, overly respectful students—students who expect to get 100% on their tests and weep if they fail at perfection. Most would never be able to pass the exams to gain admittance to overseas universities due to their poor English, but all assumed they had to study at a foreign university anyway. Money was spent on classes at this tutoring school where students took classes to learn to pass the entrance tests.

So, I was here waiting to be called into the boss's office. They liked to make you wait a bit.

I had developed some of the trepidation Thais had when dealing with a big boss. As an American, I was taught that I could be on equal footing with anyone by sporting my big white guy's grin and a handshake, but I knew that most countries had their own kind of decorum. Here in Thailand, it was the expectation that people should acknowledge and respect the innate different levels of power we were all on. And I was on the level of desperately needing my job. I wanted to be able to live out here in Thailand. I wanted to make my fortune.

My Thai boss, and all big-time Thai guys, did not have conversations. He expected to give a speech without interruption, and the employee was expected to listen and acquiesce.

Sure, there was always the garrulous Western woman who expected to be treated as an equal and have a conversation where she challenged the assertions of the Thai boss and expected to be congratulated for her confidence, but such a person would find herself afterwards forever excluded from the precincts of power, having demonstrated she did not know how to interface with top people, at least not with the Thai ones.

I listened to their speeches without interrupting, to show I knew the game. It was not cynical. I was genuinely excited to be a part of the inner circle at the top.

So, on that day, I waited nervously in the hallway outside of the big man's office.

I was not nervous, I told myself.

Maybe it was my drinking. Maybe it showed somehow as I taught my classes. But no one knew how much I was drinking. I didn't even know, but I guess I knew.

I was Bert Mars. I had been through tense and crazy things before. I should be able to handle this.

I was soon called into the high sanctum of the boss. He was sitting, presiding really, behind a massive teak desk. In such a situation, an official speech to a subordinate, he had on all his Thai seriousness—it was a seriousness bordering on sanctimoniousness and it was its own warning to take him seriously.

There was a man next to him who I had never seen before. In uniform. The boss had been known to intimidate those he thought were disloyal or crossed him, and I thought this was what was going to happen. But I was not disloyal and I was desperate and thankful for my job.

My mind prepped a defense of myself while I tried to determine what kind of uniform the man was wearing. It was hard to tell because all of the Thai bureaucracy had these uniforms with ranks and the badges and honor of tenure.

The boss then began, "I have a job for you," and explained, in the tone he used when recounting something confidential, that, a helicopter had crashed. Yes, I had heard about this in the news.

The pilot, who had guided the craft down and escaped unharmed, was the uniformed man beside him, one of the boss's school chums. Thais stuck together and maintained these educational associations for life.

I soon realized what was going on. I was not in trouble. I was being welcomed into the inner sanctum for a special mission. I was still trusted.

Apparently, a strut on the chopper had come loose during flight, and this had caused the chopper to crash. Some other explanation was going to be given officially as to why it crashed; I cannot exactly remember now.

I was being asked to pick up some money from the helicopter manufacturer and deliver it to the pilot to ensure that the real details of the crash never became public.

The reason was that, in the United States—which made all of the consequential aviation equipment during that time—liability laws were such that any hint of breakage and thus defect in an aircraft would trigger an avalanche of associated liability and lawsuits for similar events in the U.S.

Courts there accepted that incidents with real or imagined defects could be used to extract millions of dollars from manufacturers for their supposed gross negligence. It was a heyday for lawyers. Thus, it was imperative for aircraft companies to stamp out any possible avenues for increased liability.

The company that built the helicopter had sent its men over to Thailand with a briefcase full of U.S. dollars—50,000. How exactly they got the money together—brought in or supplied by a local subsidiary—I have no idea, but that was the price for the silence of the pilot. The broken strut would never be recorded as the cause of the crash.

It was not said why I was chosen to pick up the money, but I knew why. The money was being delivered by Westerners and the Thais wanted to remain apart from the mechanics of what was going on, while having a Westerner who they could totally rely on to pick up the cash. That was me.

I was inwardly elated. I was on the inside of power here again. I wasn't being fired. I was being welcomed back into the world of the Thais, who usually shielded their real thinking from judgmental Westerners with their Thai smiles.

As the details of the money pickup plan were being related to me by the big boss in the vague, roundabout ways Thais related things, the pilot eyed me suspiciously.

He was a coiled little man, somehow still and vibrant at the same time. I imagined he would be an attentive pilot. His posture was somewhat warped as he leaned forward across the desk towards me, perhaps greedy with anticipation of the windfall that he was going to earn due to his lucky crash.

I was not told to keep any of this a secret, but it was implied, like I was the right person on the right mission. I was thrilled to be in their confidence.

Had I been asked about this in front of the other teachers at the school, all foreigners like me, I might have been hesitant to wholeheartedly agree to it, feeling a bit of social pressure to display my Westerner's virtuousness, but luckily, no one ever really knew what I was up to.

Then, I was in a taxi on the way to pick up the money, not my money, but it was money.

After coming back to my job here, I had vowed not to be a part of crazy schemes anymore, but some time had passed, my fears had subsided, and I saw the wealth and fortunes to be made in the big city.

I decided it was okay to do this. To take a chance. One last time to be ambitious. I expected myself to achieve, to make my fortune, and I was here in Asia, the new land of opportunity with its days of sweltering heat and no snow.

I soon arrived at one of the best hotels in town and then went up to a hotel room.

The door opened. A youngish Westerner squinted at me. He called over his shoulder back into the room.

"Is this the right guy?" he said.

Another man appeared from behind him, putting on his glasses. My boss had told me these representatives were lawyers. They looked it.

"Aat sent me," I said. I had been told to tell them this. Aat was the name of the pilot I had met in the boss's office.

I was let in and waited in the entryway of what was obviously a suite of rooms.

One of the men, I could not really tell them apart, handed over what was by then an old-fashioned accoutrement, a briefcase. It was the kind one's father would have trudged to work with in an earlier time, filled with pencils, the papers of business, and the meager lunch of one who anticipates that hard work alone will gain them success.

In the briefcase, I could feel the heft of money.

The man started to smile at me, then stopped. It was a sudden feeling we both had that we should be businesslike, maybe have some plausible deniability.

I decided not to open the briefcase. That could be my plausible deniability—I was just the bag man.

"Okay?" he said.

"Okay," I replied and hoped it would be.

We were both here, doing these things.

He called back to the other man, "We're going to be late for our Muay Thai lessons."

The lawyers were clearly using this mission as a bit of a holiday.

The lawyers were particularly short, and, like many short men, aficionados of the martial arts. I guess this world does something to short men. A few little comments—maybe a snide remark from a girl years ago to a kid who was a couple of inches shorter than others—caused lifelong overcompensation, resulting in short martial artists. We all chase our past. I wished him well.

This was normal, I thought, as I walked away that day with the money. I imagined my own nation as a paragon and that all other nations were to be admonished to live up to its standards. But this was how it really was. I wondered if every one of my countrymen were coarse and grasping like these lawyers. Like me. It made me sad. I wanted to believe that, even if I was willing to break the rules, most would never consider such a thing. But I had learned otherwise. It was like finding out how much money your parents made and realizing that they were poor.

No one noticed me that day. I am sure no one took note of me getting into the taxi and carrying the money back, my mission accomplished.

My boss and Aat, the pilot, were waiting when I returned. They opened the briefcase and counted the money greedily, almost as if they could not believe I would bring it all back to them.

I saw their eyes. It was like the mask had fallen from my image of them as remote, unknowable Thais.

What I had brought back was not that much money, but, at the time, it was an astonishing amount to me. The pilot explained that he would not keep it all, but that it was to be divided between himself and his superiors to ensure that the broken strut was never mentioned again and another reason for the crash was agreed upon.

He was feeling happy with the money safely in hand and so he chatted with me. He proudly told me his class motto: "The sword does not ask why it is sharp." However, he did not quite have the language skills to explain its meaning.

But I understood the meaning. And it shocked me to hear the saying because I had heard it, not too long ago, at the job I had fled from in the neighboring country.

It was when I was facing terror, when I fought for my life. It was when I had decided to do bad things and barely escaped. But I did it. I had dared and I did it.

It made me know that anything was still possible in this age I was living in. Anything that could be done would be done, and perhaps that wasn't always a positive thing, but I was here, and I would find a way to make my fortune.

As I left, Aat stood up and gave me a Western-style handshake. My boss looked on, no doubt pleased he was able to show he had a foreigner who worked for him and followed his orders. The boss was happy. I was in his confidence, and I still had my job. We all felt the camaraderie that forms between brave soldiers or possibly dishonest scoundrels.

I could now see the money flowing in this place, going here and there, lots of it, chunks I could never imagine back home in my nanny state.

I knew people were not supposed to cheat. I was supposed to be a beacon of Western propriety for these little nations and their corruption. But I wanted adventure, and I did not care about teaching other people lessons. I guess they were teaching me lessons—seeing the money being made in tutoring schools, the bribes going around, and the bursting energy of business.

These lands where places of skirting and bending rules, where reputations and connections amounted to more than assumptions that rules should apply equally to all. It was almost becoming common sense to me. And this was my land now, completely alien and open, the way I liked it.

2

The delivery of the money was only a temporary distraction. It gave me just a taste of what was possible.

Now I was back to the daily drudgery of working for a living like a common sap, taking home just enough each month that I would come back the next day for more. And spending a bit more than I had each month because I knew more was coming the following month. The life of a drudge. That's how they get you.

Still, there was money here. Money all around. Knowing this ate at me like a worm. It was pernicious. There was money in the tutoring school I worked for.

I did not hate the people who were making it. I did not think the government deserved some of the money in taxes. I just thought I must have success too, and, as an American, I thought if I worked hard enough, maybe cut some corners, I could get it. It was a righteous jealousy.

At my last job in a nearby country, I became involved, for financial gain, in a scheme to unseat a government. I was even pretty sure that my own government, if not directly involved in the plot, was happy for the plan to succeed.

However, the scheme did not work. People got hurt and I got away with some money, an interesting story and lingering guilt.

My escape happened when my heart was speeding fast and events of living and dying were fresh in my mind, and what could have been lost outweighed what I thought I could have gained.

But the guilt faded. And the money was spent. And the story in my mind was retold, this time woven into an adventure with me as the hero.

Now that I was back in Bangkok, I saw the wealth again and I began to ponder what I needed to do to get ahead, a young man in an era of opportunity. I knew now that everyone who got ahead must have challenged the way things were, if not the universe itself.

An idea was growing in my mind, but I knew that I did not have the money or smarts to do it all on my own. I wanted to have a couple of partners, brothers-in-arms to fortify me through the uncertain task of starting a business. Anyone who has tried to start a business on their own will know what I mean.

Not long after, I whispered to my fellow teachers Colm and Matthew in the teachers' break room.

"Funny to be living out here and be an employee, a low-level employee," I said. "This is supposed to be an era of booming business. We need to go where the money is."

"Yes," Colm said. "I've thought of that too."

Colm was a Frenchman with an Irish name, a tangle of cultures like many of these Europeans were. His father had been a diplomat, and he had had a privileged childhood. Colm was always brainstorming, as I was, about business ideas.

"This is a once-in-a-lifetime era we are living in," I said. "We missed the gold rush, the Roaring Twenties, but we are here in Asia as it is booming. And with opportunity we could never dream of back home."

"There's money to be made," Matthew said. "Especially in tutoring schools like this one."

Matthew was usually the silent one, so I was surprised by his enthusiasm. Usually, I only heard him speak when we passed by a class where he was teaching. He was the kind of guy who joined every gathering and had a pleasant enough time, but who rarely spoke.

"Maybe we should start our own tutoring school," Colm said.

"Is it possible?" Matthew asked.

"It's possible," I said.

Colm had said what I had been thinking—what we had all been thinking—that we should strike out and set up our own school.

This was what I wanted—a wholesome business, a business I understood, and everything legal and on the level.

We knew that we, the teachers, were why the students flocked to the school. We were the revered "native speakers," perceived as having special and authentic knowledge needed for students to pass their standardized tests that allowed admissions to foreign universities.

We realized that we would be sacked if it were learned we were considering starting a new competing school. So, Colm, Matthew, and I began meeting every Wednesday after classes to work out our plans—the corporate structure, the permits, and, most importantly, the start-up money we would require.

"We're going to need a special business structure. This kind of business, a school, cannot be in a non-Thai's name," Colm said. "We will need a nominee structure to secretly control it."

I knew this was the case, but it felt uncomfortable to cede control of the business to others and not have it in our names. And we were risking our present jobs with these plans. But this is what it would take.

Colm just said, "It'll be fine."

He began pushing for us to quit our jobs and make a quick start to our school. He was grand and confident, in a way I felt I never was, so I both admired and envied him.

"We have to move fast," he said. "This is our chance. Once the company account is in place, we need to quit and get started on the new school."

"We shouldn't make any move until the nominee structure for the company is set up," Matthew said.

"It'll be fine," Colm replied, as he always did, and I sort of believed him.

Colm had a little dossier of papers about our company plans which he kept under a pulled-out desk drawer where he worked at the school. He was careful not to let anyone see him remove the drawer to retrieve the paperwork, but I saw it.

I hoped we were being clever enough.

Starting a tutoring school meant I would have to put my other business plan on hold.

The other plan was to open a beach front hotel.

I knew a Thai guy who owned some family land on the southern coast. It was really just some shacks by the beach. I was trying to convince him to lease the land to me.

He had advertised the lease at the going rate—less than a thousand U.S. dollars a month, but now that I was ready to commit, he always found some excuse to delay the commencement of the lease.

He was an indolent guy who had been raised in the States and who had been contaminated by our ways. He had never worked but lived on inheritance and land leases, all earned by his illustrious parents, who had worked themselves to death for him.

However, he was still Thai in that he regarded beachfront land as generally useless, Thais in the past not wanting to become "black" in skin color by going to the beach.

When his parents died, and their holdings were divided among their children, he had thought he was the loser of the family, as he got the useless beach land, while his sister got the valuable inland plot near an industrial area.

The land I wanted to lease was located about halfway down the coast on the Gulf of Siam. It already had a collection of run-down bungalows on it, left over from an earlier failed attempt at a business there. The whole area was in a dead zone for tourism, well beyond what was feasible for anyone in Bangkok to drive to for a weekend trip. But someone would come, I believed.

Still, it was more than that.

It was the very idea that I could have a business right on the beach. This was beyond what someone of my ken could imagine back in my own country. It could only happen here in paradise.

These business ideas—the land and the school—made my crazy decision to live in Thailand, the risks I had taken, all seem worth it. It made me feel like I was way ahead of my friends, toiling away in the cold winters back home. It made me glad I was doing all these things now when I was young and willing to take the risk. It was my victory over my place in the world and my decisions and everyone I sought to impress.

Sue, the lone female teacher among us at the tutoring school, had an opinion too. I did not know how she found out about our plans. Women had a way of finding things out.

"I know what you guys are up to. And you should know you can't get the license for a school because you're foreigners," she said.

She said this with her arms crossed like she was saying something final. Something settled.

"We've got a plan," I said.

"I know all about you. You're overconfident," she said. "And do you think the owner of this school is going to let you walk away to compete with him?"

I always hated when women judged me and were also right about it. The owner of the school, the "big boss" as we called him, did have police connections and could cause us trouble. Also, I liked him and didn't want him to think I had crossed him.

The licensing of the new school was also an issue, but it was bureaucracy and there were always ways around that.

"We'll figure it out," I said, probably with an overconfident smile.

She just sneered in disapproval.

I did not like her very much, but I somehow got the feeling she liked me, and this was her way of showing it.

Andrew, another teacher at the school, advised me against the plan too.

"No, I would not do it. No. No," he said.

His speaking was a combination of his Northern English accent—sort of a mumbled, compressed way of speaking—and his increasing dependence on too much alcohol. When he spoke, he looked to one side, as if he were receding away from me.

"It's not worth the risk," he said. "You have a job here already."

Andrew was one of my oldest friends out here. He had long ago given up on any big scheme to enrich himself. He had worked on his own school project years ago that fell apart after it came to light that he did not have the proper permits.

He was one of those ruined and brilliant men who had lost themselves in the far places of the world. He spoke several languages, including Arabic, and he was a genius at spontaneously creating original lesson material for the college-bound students we tutored. He remained in the background at the school, spinning out the lessons, year after year. Thais did not realize he was different; all foreigners were assumed to be unaccountably odd and beyond reason.

Then he began drinking more and more—same as I had. Maybe we did not realize how much we influenced each other.

"I'm going to do something," I told him. "I'm going to do this business. I'm not just going to be a teacher here forever."

"I know that," Andrew replied without looking at me, passively acceding to my claims as if he were a parent not wanting to crush my dreams.

I bragged to him about the money to be made. I told him how good the plan was.

As he was resigned to his job at the school, and no longer showed any ambition to do anything else, it felt bad to be confronting him with this.

"I can make it work." I said. "There are always ways to do things. That's why I'm here. You just have to consider if you can do what it takes."

"That's what you should be afraid of," Andrew said.

He looked up at me from behind a long lank of uncut hair. He had a tired smile. He looked every bit the genius professor who had taken to drink.

He was used to this casual and unforgiving land. Petrified in place. He could not return to his own country.

Andrew reminded me of myself, and this made me all the more determined to make my own move into a business.

Colm, Matthew and I started to worry that our plans would leak out to the school management. Sue and Andrew already knew. We had probably talked too much. We always talked too much. Things suddenly were urgent.

I had a few thousand dollars in savings—all that I had in the world. We were putting our savings together for a business that we knew how to do, and we knew had a big demand, right in this big city. In the exuberance and foolishness of the moment, it felt right and not desperate to consider risking it all, and I did not want to be left behind in what was happening. The countdown had begun. We were ready to quit once the business structure was in place and approved.

Sitting in the teachers' break room day after day, I dreamed of my bright future, while my students assumed I was carefully grading their coursework.

It seemed that the world had always taught me that there was no real getting ahead, and that I would only ever be this, a worker, watching others go by in their expensive cars while I walked to work. It was city life. I did not hate the rich. I loved them and was sure one day I would be in my own expensive car.

I wanted something to happen, and usually when I got that feeling, I went out in the evening and had a beer. This was normal, I was told, by the English, Irish, Swedish, and Australian expats I worked with. They thought it quite normal to drink as much as you wanted each night.

This was quite a difference from the puritanical American view on alcohol I had been taught, but I ended up matching the Europeans, beer for beer.

I could feel it, even now. It was not exactly physical. It was a thought, grasping here and there for relief. It was a loss of contentment. It was saying to me: What is the use of an evening without a drink?

I found myself falling asleep at the pub after our planning meetings, but there were lots of foreigners like me in Bangkok and somehow, I always got home.

It was a wonderful time that I knew I would always remember. We were young men working on our big plans. I wanted something to happen, and I was tired of waiting.

3

Then, one day, Colm did not show up for work at the school. Then another day and another, and a weekend passed and neither Matthew nor I could contact him.

We went to our bank—the bank where we had pooled our money for the school in an account we were all supposed to sign off on.

The account was empty.

I returned to the school break room.

"Why are you moping around?" Sue asked.

I had not thought I was betraying my feelings to her. I dejectedly admitted that our money was gone.

She laughed in the "I told you so" way some people do—I guess in the way I would have, had I not been the one who was in this position.

"Everything here's set up against small fry like you," Sue said. "I told you."

"Maybe," I said. "But I'll figure this out." I said it like I was mad and determined, but was saying this to myself in the haze of the foolishness I found myself in.

"Thailand doesn't give you anything. It only takes," she said. "It can work if you pay them. You are a rich foreigner to them. You deserve to be cheated."

"It wasn't Thailand," I said. "It was Colm."

Sue went silent for a moment.

"I knew this wouldn't work out," she said. "Better report him."

In a daze, Matthew and I filed a complaint with the local police and the French embassy, going through the process like zombies. It was paperwork and then it was done. It was a pointless exercise. No one was interested. I felt more foolish than ever.

Matthew blamed me.

"You were the head of this," he said accusingly. But I had thought Colm had been in charge.

"How could you let this happen? I knew you were the wrong person for this job," he said. "Crazy to trust a foreigner out here."

"I can't really argue with that," I told him.

I knew how much it took to rouse Matthew to say more than a few words at a time, and he said it to me with an involuntary sneer. It was humiliating.

That afternoon at the school, I received a call. It was Colm.

"What's going on?" I said. "The account's empty! You're gone?" I was saying all the things we both already knew.

"Bert, I called you. Only you," he said gravely. "I know your history. Maybe you can understand this."

"What are you talking about?" I said.

"This is too big to really explain, and I had no choice. But this was the one time, the one time I could do this, and I'm going to try to find it. You will get your money back and more besides and we will start our school back in Bangkok. I promise. It's all crazy. I know that!"

"What are you talking about? Find what?"

"You'll have to trust me," he said, "Look. We are close to finding it. It's here. Don't worry. It'll be fine."

"We who? What are you talking about? Where are you?" But he had hung up. And I could hear the faint empty static on the analog line.

Colm had fooled me and taken advantage of me for some reason. But it was a very minor scam—for not a lot of money—not a huge amount. But maybe enough for someone to at least be tempted.

All day, I had that sick empty ego feeling, when you realize you are not as smart as you think you are. It is the feeling that says you cannot sneer at all the dummies who usually fall for these things, as now you are one of them.

Sue was watching, as always, as I sat in the breakroom. She was kind of my conscience, I guess. I got the feeling she wanted to be my girlfriend, but I wasn't interested.

"You like to think you are above everything, but this proves you're not," she said.

I thought that this was a nasty thing to say, but I just said, "Yeah."

Sue looked a bit disappointed I had accepted her appraisal without arguing. I did not want to show I was upset in front of her, so I tried to look tough.

"You guys don't know what you are doing," she added, trying again.

She was watching me. I thought she was testing my reaction. See what kind of man I was.

"It's your life," she said. "Anyway, you should have taken my advice."

"Why not think I am above it all?" I said. "That's not a bad ambition."

She didn't like that. But she turned a critical eye on us, and young men don't like that either. Or perhaps we cannot bear it. I was glad I was not her boyfriend.

I walked home that day too ashamed to show I was mad. And I was too mad to admit I had failed. I had to go home to my little room and let it sink in.

My rented room wasn't a home or even an apartment, really, but just a box where I kept my belongings to prevent them from blowing away in the wind.

I started to feel insulted by it all. Why did Colm call me? To put me off searching for him? Was he just a nut? Like me?

The universe stops you. No, it was me, but I was the universe, a series of unconscious things that tended to happen, caused by the kind of dumb person I was. All this had led me here. Things are always as hard as they can possibly be.

My hand was on my shirt over the necklace I wore. It was a little blood-red amulet, a tiny Buddhist image, given to me by a former girlfriend, who I had carelessly abandoned and only remembered when I felt for the amulet in times of trouble.

Many people wore these amulets in Thailand, and shops sold them everywhere, often purported to be from ancient times. I tried to take comfort from such beliefs, but I could not. What was happening was something about my ego and foolishness.

I finally had done things the right way and I got myself cheated. I would not have cheated someone else like this. Something was wrong here, or maybe it wasn't. Maybe that was the issue. Maybe I did not realize how things tended to be. One way or another, I was the fool.

This event took the edge off my happiness. Colm had smiled in my face and I had believed him.

4

Around this time, Andrew suddenly quit. He had been working at the school the longest of us all.

I had thought Andrew was content in his passive working life, buried far away from his own country, but Andrew had friends on the border on the Mekong, visiting them every long weekend. He had come back from his last trip, uncharacteristically verbose, explaining that he had met a boatman who told him that U.S. POWs were still being held in the jungles.

"A man in a boat, a boat," he mumbled. "They got POWs there."

This was absurd. These countries were vast and had their remoteness, but all had governments eager to do business with the West. It was inconceivable that any of them would have wanted to hold Western captives after all these years.

Most of the teachers at the school, myself included, had been to the areas he was referring to when we went over the border to renew our Thai visas.

It was industrial parks and endless developments on each side of the river, concrete shophouses, and vacant lots awaiting development, strewn with plastic bags that swirled in the wind like a tornado. It was hard to believe any secret camp could be in the area.

But Andrew's friend had a boat, and Andrew was going across the river to search for POWs.

"This is important," he said.

"It's not important," I replied. "It's impossible."

"No. It's important to do something worthwhile," he said.

He gestured, and the way he did it made me think he was contrasting his new mission with our jobs at the school.

Yeah, I knew just working here was a road to nowhere for just a salary, spending it all and a little bit more each month because I counted on more coming. But it wasn't the lesson I thought I would learn from Andrew. I thought I was the smart visionary.

And I couldn't make a claim to be a smart visionary after I had let myself get cheated.

Andrew gave his notice at the school, and, with backpack slung over his shoulder, shook hands with me in a manly way and told me to look him up if I ever got up there. I said I would, and he was gone.

I wasn't sure why he wanted to find POWs, but he had found his mission, and it had led him away from the school, ahead of me.

When I had quit the school once in the past, Andrew had told me that I would be back at the school teaching again, and, when I came crawling back, I realized he had been right.

Now, Andrew, the least among us, was moving on, but I was still stuck here, penniless.

I wondered if I could really see who he was outside of my own thoughts on his drinking. I had misjudged Colm too. I wondered how many others I had not perceived correctly.

I was on a knife's edge, down to my last baht each month, but I took comfort in being far away from anyone who judged me. It was back when you could do that, when people communicated by postcards from places like this. It was a place for people who didn't want to say much, and who didn't want to say how they were doing.

So many fell into the trap of years of teaching in an apparent paradise, making very little. And then they were old, and if they had to go back to their home country, they did not know how to be old there. This was the life of the expat forced back into his own kind—back into the hermetical life of the old in the West—the true definition of culture shock.

I considered this involuntarily as I noticed my own reflection in the windows of the school. All the Westerners working here were weird garbage. I did not want to be a fool. I had thought that I was the smart one and depended on that assumption.

5

A woman appeared one day, as they always seemed to. Maybe it is just that men notice these things.

She arrived at the school and spoke to a few people before she approached me.

"You were Colm's best friend, I hear?" she asked.

"I don't think so. Maybe," I said. I was still in the grips of my anger over the loss of my money.

"Do you know where he is?"

"No."

She paused, as if expecting more of an answer, then continued.

"I'm Lori, his sister. His mother, our mother, is very worried. As you may know, our father died recently. Our mother is sick, and, as you know, he's impulsive."

I knew Colm was from a Catholic family, one of those families with many, many kids, most now estranged from their frazzled mother, apparently grown crazy from doing her duty to produce more Catholics.

"He left suddenly," I said. "I wish I knew where he was."

"Coming out here..." Lori said, pausing uncertainly. "He's always trying some get-rich-quick scheme. His mother just wants to find him."

A perfect tear formed at the corner of her eye. It was in that seductive way women cry when they are tempting you to sympathize and protect them. Even knowing this, it made me want to help her.

I laughed a bit.

"What's so funny?" she said, mock offended.

"I'm as sad he's gone as you are," I said.

She looked at me quizzically.

"Look, I have some theories maybe, but I don't know where he is," I said.

"I just returned from there," she said. "And I can't find him."

"There?" I said, perking up.

Lori then told me the name of the country she had just returned from.

I knew something now. A real clue.

And, knowing this, I knew even more than that. More than she knew or anyone knew. This was because, once I had realized that the company account had been emptied, I had gone to Colm's apartment.

His room had been empty, the door ajar, as they often were here, in preparation to rent to the next tenant.

I found the bank of mail slots for the building. There was a single letter there addressed to Colm—an envelope peeking out of a slot. I could see from the return address that it was from a local law firm. I didn't feel the need to justify anything at this point. Indeed, this was a country where no one ever had to justify themselves. I did not even look around but took the letter and walked away.

The letter was a reply to Colm's inquiry about setting up a holding company—apparently in a neighboring country—but it did not say which country.

The message read: "Legal & Accounting Services: Khamsone Company, with Foreign Holdings Corp 49% shareholder and 51% (local nominee)." The invoicing item was "foreign financial services," meaning it was not in Thailand.

I had the letter in my pocket when I spoke to Lori and I had told no one about it. I had pondered taking it to the police or the French Embassy, but neither had been interested in helping me get my money back thus far.

And now Lori had told me the country that this company must be located in. Now I knew something.

"Can you go up on the long weekend and check?" she said. "I'll pay for your ticket and room."

This was perfect. The upcoming weekend was one of the many long weekends that these little countries had. This one was a holiday with both Friday and Monday off and the school I worked at would be closed.

It was a chance to redeem myself, if only in my own eyes. I was going to get my money back. It was a righteous mission now.

"I have a message for him from his mother," she said. "Can you give it to him?"

She handed me an envelope. It clearly had a piece of paper folded inside. I wouldn't be carrying any drugs or contraband.

I looked at her. She paused, awaiting my reply. She was not beautiful, but beautiful enough. You know the type. A face one would remember in a good way.

For some reason, I held back in telling her my issue with Colm—him running away with the money. Maybe she already knew. But I did not want to reveal anything that I did not have to reveal.

"Okay. I'll see if I can find him," I said, suppressing my excitement.

"I have a feeling you are going to find him," she said with the upmost sincerity. "You are the right person for this."

She had that confidence—that I was in her power because she was a woman. If she were prettier, I would have scoffed at this. However, she was just pretty enough to be intriguing and just old enough to know a few things. It was the right balance of everyday looks and confidence, and it made me willing to go along with her request. Maybe it was a path back to my money.

I had a few big bottles of beer that night—the cheap local kind that left a sour taste on your teeth. It always clarified things. Normally, I would worry about several things, but after drinking, this would automatically narrow down to one thing—and I would be able to see a way, not only to succeed, but to triumph.

I would confront Colm. Get my money back. Maybe I would rough him up, but he had been my friend, after all, lying, cheating scammer that he was.

I realized how drinking made me think differently. I got the feeling it made my decisions 2% off. So, it was nothing, really, barely any effect on any day—slightly late to work, putting off something important, running down my health a bit. But then, after a time, that 2% added up and would steer me off course.

Still, I was going to try, even though the universe works against you, especially when you try to do big things.

6

This was happening almost at the end of adventure. The world was nearly knit together by internationalization and trade agreements and technology, with just a few places still remote.

Airports were the opposite of adventure. It was the going through of a funnel, all regulated people, regulated down to our possessions, and the spelling of our legal names on documents. An airport was a bureaucratic exercise to prevent anything unusual or notable from happening. It was a series of standing in lines, of letting them know the exactitude of your coming and going.

Airports gave me a vague sense of dread, of loneliness when leaving one place and going to another.

I had the feeling that someday, an airport would be my undoing—the undoing of my luck—the one thing I knew I had.

I sat there on the hard plastic chairs, gripping my travel documents, thinking with all the others around me of where I was going to end up and why I was going there.

This was my mission.

Nothing was going to make me support a government, worry about a recession, or fight a war. I wanted no cause. I had never donated, never volunteered, never put a coin in a cup, never heeded the call to march after someone else's indignation.

Maybe it was from living outside the country of my birth for so long in places where you can never be one of them. When, after a time, you become nothing, really—just a forever in-between.

But I could always go on, another airplane, another land. There was always a fresh new world that did not care about me. They were all self-contained anyway, seeing nothing beyond their borders.

This was something I would never say out loud to anyone else, but I knew it deeply within my heart, and now you know it too.

So, this is what happened, how it started, which is true as far as I know, or maybe a distortion, what I believe to be true, through my imperfect eyes. It is my context, just as I saw all my impossibly smart students at the school and they saw me as their perfect revered teacher.

It was a busy Friday afternoon when I arrived in the foreign capital, the sun punishing as it always is in such places.

The capital was like a provincial town back in Thailand and had a sleepy aura over it. It was too far away from any sea. Its wide well-planned boulevards lay in the sun, perplexed and waiting for traffic. Some people, older, lean and dark, moved deliberately in the sun, manning food carts. It was a slow-motion world, unsuitable for my paleness, but I had long ago become accepting that my fortune would be made in a place like this and I would endure it.

I went directly to a street known to be frequented by tourists and those few who worked in the capital. Westerners who came to this country were exotic foreign things, made for a different kind of climate, and needed this place to congregate and survive.

There were a few expats and local girls there, all jumbled together on this street. Were the local girls looking for boyfriends? Maybe they were regular and respectable. It was hard to judge people from outside of my own culture. And then there was always a smattering of hip local youngsters who wanted to hang out with the international scene.

It would be the right place for Colm. He was a sociable carouser, like those European types often were. It would have saved a lot of trouble to find him here. I had a vague hope I would see him, but thought, since people were looking for him, that would be unlikely.

Andrew had mentioned this street and his friend's pub here. And he *was* there.

He did not know me at first, then slowly realized who I was, his brain sorting through information to recognize me.

"Oh! Oh, hi. You're here!" Andrew said, as if I had told him I was coming, and he had forgotten somehow.

He looked terrible, the geography of life on his face, craggy in the sun.

At first, Andrew said he had not seen Colm, then later in conversation he said, "Yes. I know where he is," but seemed to confuse this with his search for POWs. "Yes, they are there, but I am sworn to secrecy! Believe me, I will find them!"

It is disturbing when someone you know acts crazily knowing they have done it to themselves through their habits.

"You know that Colm ran off with our money," I said. "That's why I'm here."

Andrew, peering out of his drunkenness said, "It was worth a try." He said it in a kindly way, but it embarrassed me, having another show this pity.

Maybe he noticed this, because he changed the subject by proudly showing me a lighter.

"This proves it," he said. "A soldier's lighter."

It was a Zippo lighter. There were legions of them left here—relics of a time when U.S. soldiers flooded the region.

An engraving on one side read:

Lucky by day
Lucky by night
I should have ducked
Shit out of luck.

A three-headed mythological elephant was on the other side with the word "Erawan."

The engraving was done by hand, awkward, rustic.

All these sorts of lighters had the crude, cynical sayings of American farm boys who had never heard of where they were going when they were first sent out here, and when masculine smoking was part of being a man in war.

The silver shell of the lighter was rough and had been scraped a million times as it was taken in and out of a pocket while the security of smoke melded with the uncertainty of war.

I imagined the face of the soldier every time he lit his cigarette, the light both illuminating the words and his face for a moment.

But it was probably a fake. I had seen cabinets of them in Saigon, laboriously engraved with the folksy sayings of the Yanks.

"A man told me he would guide me up to the hills," Andrew said. "There's a trail to a village and there's an old man there who knows about a secret camp."

"This is a scam," I said. "There's no way these countries wanting to trade with the rest of the world would be secretly holding POWs."

"Oh, no. They are just living there voluntarily. They gave it all up or were shell shocked. It's a hidden village—just old soldiers farming in the hills."

It sounded attractive. Being a reprobate in the jungle, giving up on challenges, giving up on ambition.

There was animation in Andrew's face. He was enraptured by his quest, and I hated throwing cold water on it. He needed a mystery, I guess. His own chance to be lucky. Drinking makes you the person that you think you are, but you know you're not.

"I'm going to liberate them. Find them. Send them home," he said.

"But what if they do not want to go back?" I replied.

Andrew looked at me and then back to his drink.

"Yeah," was all he said.

I looked again at the Zippo lighter sitting on the table—an artifact of my people in this land, or perhaps a fake, made to entice me into believing it was real.

I was going to get my money back from Colm, one way or another.

"So, what are you doing up here other than searching for POWs?" I asked.

"I'm looking for a job," Andrew replied, and we both laughed. The difference between heaven and hell is often just a bit of regular money.

It dawned on me that being here, so far away, doing this vague thing, was not good for me. Perhaps it was the beginning of a story where the hero ended up dead, having made foolish choices he suspected were wrong.

I finished my beer and ordered another. It was one of the delicious, sweet, cheap local beers. It was unusually refreshing in the heat. It was a strange life we had chosen, becoming buried here in the everlasting sun.

A couple of odd birds we were. We had found the right place in the world.

7

It was not as easy as I thought. I had envisioned Colm
would be around here, sitting in one of the pubs, waiting
for his confrontation with me. Andrew had probably not
really seen him, but through his muffled speech and
thinking, it was impossible to know.

My next move was to find Colm's company. I had with
me the lawyer's letter I had retrieved from Colm's
apartment in Bangkok that stated the name of his company.
I guessed it had to be here in this city, the only sizeable city
in this country.

Andrew helped me get a taxi. He already had a strong command of the local language which I was envious of.

The taxi driver, an old man in a late-model U.S. car, seemed to know the address from the lawyer's letter.

We rumbled along. The car smelled like exhaust inside. Combined with the hot sun, it became an otherworldly and slightly dizzy ride—a hot Friday at the end of the world.

The neighborhoods we passed were a consistently jumbled mix of shophouses hugging the side of the road, mini mansions peeking over high walls topped with broken glass set in concrete, and factories and warehouses of all sizes. Zoning would have to wait for another generation.

Here and there were signs with familiar international brands such as Bridgestone tires, but the text was in the lyrical local script.

The streets teemed, with not a single Mercedes like in Bangkok, but with all means of foot-powered transportation. Bicycles and rickshaw-like vehicles rattled themselves and their passengers through the city. A few loud imported motorcycles also roamed the streets, always in a hurry to get to where they were going.

On some streets, massive, brutish trees stood their ground, and motorcycles and bicycles had to make their way around their dense canopies.

Then, the place I was looking for. It was a medium-sized, four-story building. As it was with all these buildings, it was hard to tell whether it was vacant or occupied, or in the process of moving in or out. It was the essential nature of business, rising and falling, all moving nearer to success or failure, but with no one quite sure exactly at what point until it was too late.

On the streetside were trucks and motorcycles and the men who accompanied them. Like the men who once accompanied horses, they were all a set, and several turned their heads slowly as this foreigner exited the car and entered the building.

It was as hot inside as it was outside, but at least it was out of the sun. No one was in sight. Several hard plastic chairs and a tall reception desk sat inside the door. Construction plans hung on the wall. Beyond was a darkened hallway. It was empty and silent.

I paused for a moment, considering whether to call out or not, but then decided to walk down the dark hall.

I passed a conference room and another large room with three desks. The room was probably for accounting. Papers and ledgers were stacked on the desks. There were several filing cabinets with drawers left partially open. In those days, everything was in paper form and had to be filed.

The place was a cocoon, destined to stand long after the humans who had inhabited it had moved on, and here was the paperwork they left, so critical on a single day, now pathetic in the still air.

This was the place to look for something, a clue. I was not sure what I was expecting, maybe for Colm to round the corner at any time.

Something drew me down the hall towards a shaft of light coming out of a room.

I knew Colm valued the status of having the big boss's office—he had wanted to be the headmaster of the school we were planning. Just thinking about it made me feel foolish now. But he had spoken of an office for himself needed at the school and I had detected a note of innocent vanity in his request. The room I was moving towards would likely be in a prime location for the boss's office. And I was right.

The room was clearly for the head executive of the company. There was a huge wooden desk covered in papers in the center and a high-backed chair with its back turned to me. I moved quickly to it, spinning it around dramatically, but no one was seated there.

A window looked out on a parking lot where excavation equipment was lined up.

On the wall was a photo of a man standing before what looked like a colonial-era villa in a forest. The man looked just like Colm, but from another age, with long 1970s-era hair and sideburns. It must have been Colm's father.

I stopped and listened. All quiet in the building. I opened the drawers in the desk. Generalized junk of office work. Remembering Colm's method of hiding papers in his desk at the school, I pulled out the bottom left drawer. Nothing. Then the other side.

Sure enough, there was a file folder of papers in a folder underneath. I took them out just as I heard footsteps coming down the hall.

I panicked, not having a place to put the papers, so I discarded the file folder the papers were in, and stuffed the papers into my pocket. I looked up, just as a girl, or a lady, it was hard to tell, appeared in the doorway.

She was holding a gun on me—some kind of shotgun. She held it kind of casual, like she was used to pointing a gun.

I could have been startled, and normally I would have been, but something in her face, her eyes, made me smile inwardly, intrigued.

"Did he send you?" she said, gesturing with the gun. She held it lightly like someone skilled at hitting their target.

She was the beautiful brown of the people here, as rich in golden brown color as I was a pasty white. She looked young, as so many of the locals did to me, but the confidence of her voice made me realize she was used to speaking with foreigners directly and not with the soft, diffident tone most in this region of the world did.

"No. He didn't send me," I replied. "You looking for him too? For money?"

Might as well be direct.

"You talk fast," she said.

"I try to talk slow," I said, mocking her gently.

She seemed to like this, I think.

She looked at me with a sharpness that made me realize something was wrong between her and Colm. Still, she stood at the door, hesitating to come in.

I sat down in the desk chair like I was meant to be there. I was a bit scared of her, but I had been held at gunpoint before.

"Come on in," I said, like I owned the place.

She lowered the gun and walked in confidently. As she came closer, I could see she was sizing me up.

"You know how to hold a gun," I said.

"I can shoot it too," she replied.

She sat casually on the edge of the desk, challenging me. I was still uncertain about her, but she was smiling at me now—in a serious way.

"He's not here," she said. "And everyone here has not been paid."

She was leveling with me now, I could tell. She did it in a sassy way I rarely saw out here. I think I grinned a bit at that, because she smirked back at me before continuing.

"He set up the company and then was gone. It didn't even last a month. We thought he was sincere. A good son. Coming back with his father's ashes."

I looked up, maybe with a look of surprise, and she reached across the desk. Among the cluttered items was a silver canister. She gently tapped on it.

"He didn't even bother to take it. I thought he would come back for it sometime. The employees have been taking turns staying here at the office in hopes of catching him. Now it's bad luck."

"Bad luck?"

"That he's left his father here," she said, gesturing to the urn. "He always said, 'It'll be fine.'"

Yeah, that was Colm.

"He still owes us salary," she said, as if I would have forgotten.

He was willing to cheat us all for this company and then run away. This company, my money, these employees—were all a means to an end.

Still at gunpoint, I tried to be cool.

"I just want my money from him," I said. "Just like you."

"He owes you too?" she said.

"Yeah."

I did not explain more. She seemed to accept this. She looked me over like I was an amusing animal in a zoo.

"So, who are you?" she said.

"Bert Mars," I said.

She relaxed a bit.

"You looked dangerous," she said.

"So did you," I replied.

She smiled a curious, relaxed smile like she was bored with me. It only made her more mysterious.

Neither beautiful nor plain, she was somehow plainly perfect, and the more I looked at her, the more I wondered at her. It was a grand plainness and delicateness of line in her face, the sort that might become more serenely beautiful over the years.

"You tell him that Deuan is looking for him," she said. "We all are."

I started to say, "I'm as mad as you are," but from the front of the building down the hall, there was a frantic thunder of scuffling feet coming towards the office.

I could tell then that this was not a friendly sound barreling towards this room.

Suddenly, three burly men, well, burly for the locals, flowed into the room, all eyeing me.

They looked like employees of the company. They were all wearing light blue uniforms—the kind the locals always wore in business here and always faded by the local sun from the original deep blue. Deuan said something to them in the local language.

I think she told them I was to be detained or maybe beaten up, I did not know which.

They came around both sides of the desk at me. I shoved one back violently. Then I hopped up and slid over the desk, passing by Deuan, whose expression never changed.

I ran back down the dark hall and out the front door and onto the bright street.

My driver was still there. I slipped into the taxi, and we drove off before the men got out to the street. I looked back and could see them looking about, wondering where I had gone.

I imagined Deuan peering out the door down the hall at me as I fled. I would have liked to talk to her more. She seemed nice.

8

After the revolution, years had passed and tourists were eventually welcomed back. Symbols of the old days and the old regime were converted into hotels for them.

My hotel was one such converted place. It was an old palace, or what passed for a palace in olden times. To my eyes, it was just a sprawling, creaky old house.

The ceilings were high, and the floors were wide-planked burnished wood. It was almost soothing to walk on—a giving, soft wood, no doubt made from the giant trees that once covered the land, but that now could rarely be found.

It was somewhat dark inside, and that immediately set it apart from brightly-lit modern places. I could imagine the generations of families that once lived here. I could almost hear them whispering quietly in the dimness as I was shown to my room by a square-faced young woman, impeccably dressed in an old-style wrap-around sarong. She had that perfect, impenetrable face that those recruited to work at higher-class tourist places had. She was someone cast into the role to represent what the nation thought of itself.

Once in my room, I had a beer—one of the expensive ones from the mini bar. I was exhausted from the day and didn't want to wander about in the late afternoon sun searching for a shop. It was conveniently right here. No need to resist it. I needed it, I admitted to myself. It would be clarifying. I had to think of what to do now. I had to try something. If I didn't, the universe would just lie there, smirking at me.

I sat on my four-poster bed, crammed into the small room, with walking space around it. The room was nice enough, but this was clearly some tiny chamber of the old palace that had been converted into another hotel room to generate money.

This was a place meant for tourists who wanted to experience the real country—with air-conditioning, old-fashioned chandeliers and attentive local staff—anything to be protected from the heat and dust of the streets right outside, sterile and ready for any purpose for those who would need it, each with their own minor pursuits that seemed monumental at the time. It was like looking at the stars—it always made me feel small and remote—just one tiny thing happening in this vast time.

My deep reptile brain started to speak to me, telling me I was happy that Colm hadn't succeeded, and that his business here had opened with fanfare and then closed in defeat.

Then my higher brain told me that it was a terrible thing to think. I had my own failures. And I was such a sap, that if I had met him there, and he had been amiable and offered me a job, I would surely have swallowed my bile and taken it. This must be what it is like to be a grown-up, what my father and his father had to endure—sometimes knuckling under for your own good. Knowing what side your bread is buttered on. So I was here in this far place, in this hot city, wondering how broadly I would smile once I found an opportunity.

I started looking over the papers I had taken from Colm's desk.

They were photos and documents in the local language. One was a photo of a gate with a road beyond, leading to an estate of some kind. There was text in the local language written at the bottom. The text was somewhat like Thai, but it looked slightly jollier, more vintage, somewhat noble. Maybe it was just the font style.

On the back was English writing, probably a translation of the text. It read, "Oungkran Province, see the gold moon—it will be given to the right person."

There were also receipts or invoices, all in the local language. On several, the only English language was a signed name "Louis Lambert." This was, no doubt, Colm's father. It was written in a spindly script, and I wondered at the odds, after all these years, of this document finding its way to me.

My resentment of Colm was rising again. He had taken my money, and made a move to do something, maybe something big. It was the very thing I wanted to do, that I should have been doing, and he had showed me up. All this was turning a mirror upon myself, and I didn't like it.

I laughed at myself. It was all I could do.

There were other papers about the holding company and the nominee that allowed Colm to control the company. All these little countries did that—they made laws preventing foreigners from owning companies and land. However, they allowed locals to stand in as nominees to hold the majority of the company, on paper only, so that foreigners could really own the business, as well as grand residences they could never afford back in their own country—anything for the money to flow in.

Also among the papers was a French newspaper clipping about Colm's father. He had apparently been an aide to royalty, years ago before the revolution.

There was another newspaper clipping on yellowed paper—a photo of a delicate-looking crown with a large gem in its brow.

The caption read: "The fabled crown and its grand pale blue sapphire known as the Moon Gemstone."

Someone tapped on the door. I looked through the peephole. The sun was going down for that day. A bird, for some reason, was pecking at the door. When I opened the door, it was gone. I could see that the failing light of the day was shining on the peephole glass and turning it into a golden orb of light. The bird was probably some kind of tropical magpie, pointlessly banging on my door at the glowing marble of the peephole in the late afternoon sun.

The phone rang. I answered and whoever was calling hung up.

I lay down on the bed. I always got tired earlier in these tropical climes. I watched the glowing peephole fade. I think I fell asleep.

There was more tapping on the door. I jumped up from the bed and opened the door to scare the bird away. But before me stood a man. Pleasant enough. Just looking at me. And then he forcefully stepped in and closed the door behind him. And I saw he had a small gun at his side. It all happened so fast, I didn't have time to react.

He was a dark local man in a Western-style business suit, one I imagined who had studied hard and gone to university overseas, but ended up back here, in this sunny backwater. He was a little man, one who looked like he might have been picked on for being little, and this had made him dangerous.

The man said, "What are you doing here? Tell me."

"I'm just a tourist," I said.

"You've been asking about someone, no?"

"Yes," I replied. "He owes me money."

This confused him. Or maybe it was that I was not showing any fear, but I was still waking up from my nap. I'd be scared later.

I decided to annoy him further.

"Do you know where he is?" I said this in my most innocent and sincere way.

This agitated him, and he grimaced and rubbed his hand across the back of his sweaty neck in apparent frustration.

Then he gestured with his gun, backing me up.

He dumped out my suitcase, opened a few cabinets in the room. There weren't many places to hide things in here. My suitcase contained the general clutter of an itinerant traveler. He ignored the papers I had taken from Colm's desk. He was looking for something else. He kept his gun on me.

"Where is it?" he said to himself. He gestured to me with the gun.

"What are you looking for?" I asked.

This seemed to surprise him a bit.

Only now was I fully waking up. It was an alarming spot I was in, and I suddenly felt the cowardice of self-preservation that says: Just don't get shot, no matter what. But at the same time, this person did not feel threatening, even with the gun. But he still had the gun.

"If you were sent here... you were his friend, no?" he asked.

"I'm trying to find him for his sister," I replied.

"Sister?" he said. I could see he was weighing me now, figuring how smart I was. "It could not be his sister."

He lowered his gun, almost defeated.

"With so many people he owes, I wonder what the chance is that he can pay," I said.

I was making him think.

"He doesn't have it yet," the man said to himself, referring to me.

He turned to me and said, "It's not money." And after a moment, added, "Not directly. It's the company."

The man sat down on the edge of the bed. He looked at me sadly. Then he put his hand thoughtfully to his chin.

"We will pay you more," he said, looking at me earnestly.

"Pay for what?"

Another suspicious look for me.

"If you find Colm Lambert for us, if you find what he is searching for first, we will pay you more than she will."

All this talk about payment was piquing my interest. Lori had said nothing about payment.

"Pay for what?"

He took a pad from the bedside. He looked around as if there might be others who would see. He drew a shape. It was like the crown in the news clipping I had taken from Colm's desk.

"It has a gem—a sapphire—in its brow: a pale blue gem. Like the moon. The moon that comforts us, peeking over the hilltops in our land. Excuse me, I am quoting from an old song. Old folk song."

He almost hung his head in some reverie for a moment, and then became enthusiastic.

"This marvelous thing. Long have we sought it. It is something we lost along with the old country and the old regime. It was important once. It is important now," he added, correcting himself.

Then he was back to wariness. "We dare not even possess a photo of it. You are not aware of this?"

I did not want to let on what I knew.

"No." I tried to say it innocently. "A crown?"

"Yes, a diadem with the Moon Gemstone. The gem symbolizes the full moon, shining over the land. It confers great power. If people realize it has been found, things can happen. It has meaning for the people. It is a hope for change."

"Change this one-party state?" I asked.

"We dare not speak it," he said.

"Was it your men who burst in at the company today?"

"No, but we were watching. The men on the street— many people watching. There are many, the government, who do not want it to come to light and others who want to bring it to light—bring about a new revolution." He spoke the last word almost silently, as if someone might overhear.

"And others who just want it for its value?" I asked.

"It is... valuable," he said, his voice trembling a bit. "That is why I am here. I represent those who wish to obtain it."

"So, Colm knows where it is?"

"We were hoping you could shed light on that. His father, recently deceased," he crossed himself, "certainly was adjacent to events at the time—the time of the revolution when the crown vanished. Your friend arrived at this time, and the old company, his father's, was revived. What exactly was Colm doing with the company, do you know?"

"No," I said. "Just that he set it up and cleared out, leaving his staff unpaid."

"Find him or direct us to the crown, and you will be rewarded," he said.

"Who is us?"

He leaned in and spoke like I was now his best friend.

"Collectors... and patriots," nodding like he was telling a story to a child. "Those like yourself in search of what has been lost." He laughed.

"Who does not want such a thing? If you can obtain the crown, you will be paid! I am Maurice," he said, almost triumphantly. He gave my hand an enthusiastic but weak handshake.

"American?" he asked, eagerly.

"Yes, American," I said. "I'm Bert Mars."

Suddenly, he was my friend, confiding in me.

"Such things we speak of are important and thus dangerous in a land like this where one party seeks all that is important for itself. Do not believe anyone who professes to help you," he said.

"Like people busting into my room with a gun?"

"My sincere apologies. I am sometimes ... audacious. But I am a gentleman, educated in your great land. I know what you have there—political parties, voting, labor unions, real newspapers that can criticize the government."

His eyes were wide in amazement, as if he were describing the immensity of the Grand Canyon.

"You are perhaps ignorant of the life for most here— the men farming on the steep, infertile hills. Their toil. Their life is the very embodiment of a lack of power. Those who could not dare to step into this wooden mansion..." he looked around the room, "...once an old palace—a palace in a new classless society that relegates most men, powerless, to the hinterlands. Farmers resisting when their land is flooded for hydroelectric projects—for electricity for other nations.

"To be a revolutionary is to be periodically ashamed of your own land and your own people who have created vested interests to oppress you. Year after year, the boot becomes not only heavier, but more comfortable. It is exactly the intent of the long march of a government to smooth out one's feeling of oppression over time. It hurts the deep pride knowing the land is under a yoke.

"This thing," he leaned forward and spoke in a whisper, "this crown is hope for us. It is hope that we can advance and be like you."

I felt the depth of his sentiment, his innocent admiration for my own land and its chaotic freedoms. Freedoms that selfish ambitious young men like me from free lands take for granted and even scorn.

"Contact us first. Not the government," he said. "We are dependable. Do not try to get it out of the country yourself. It must not be lost to the government."

I paused to show I was processing this information, and I wanted to make it seem like I was composing a sincere response.

"Okay. I will try," I said. "How do I contact you?"

"We will find you." Realizing this sounded sinister, he clarified. "We are watching. Don't worry. We will recompense you. We are capitalists."

He said the last word proudly in a knowing whisper.

"My dear fellow, something about you has made me confide in you," he added, chuckling to himself.

He stood up to leave, still pointing the gun. I quickly put my hand on the gun and pushed it down and away from me. I wanted to be a tough guy, but it did not seem quite right in dealing with this sort of sincere person.

"Don't point a gun at me again," I said in a voice I tried to make tough and friendly at the same time. "I've been held at gunpoint twice today."

"My pardon." He nodded his head a bit. He was a man from another time, stuck in this remote world, festering away.

"I must bid you adieu," he said, moving to the door. "Believe me in what it means to this land you are just passing through."

It was challenge to a crass Westerner to generate a genuine feeling for this far land. Unfortunately for Maurice, I was not such a Westerner. I could pass through without feeling much. That might even be for the best.

As if reading my mind, he cocked his head and quietly said, "I too serve, as we all do, yet I follow my own follies."

"I know what you mean," I said.

He tipped his hat as he left.

I got the sense that Maurice was a proud, maybe desperate revolutionary. A revolution was always unlikely, but I could not know the depths of feeling these men had. Maybe it was the same dream that I had—the hope that something great could happen to me.

I knelt down to my suitcase and roughly scooped my things back in. I noticed the envelope from Lori I was to give to Colm in the netting pocket on the inside of the suitcase. I had carried it around but had forgotten about it until now.

Now I wanted to see exactly what it said. I pulled it out and now, without hesitation, I opened it. Inside was a single folded sheet of paper. A message read, "Colm, Contact me immediately. It is in your best interests. Don't try to do this alone," and then a phone number. It was signed, "Sanders."

It did not appear to be a note from Colm's mother as Lori had claimed.

I pocketed the papers from Colm's office along with the letter and went down to the concierge. I pulled out a city map brochure (they had those in those days) from a small stand there and looked at the names of hotels and their phone numbers listed on one side. There were just a handful of hotels, as no cut-rate guest houses were yet allowed.

I scanned down the list and quickly found the number that matched Lori's note—"Luxury Hotel." It was the type of bland and direct name a non-English speaker might choose as a name that accurately advertises a hotel's assumed virtues.

Years later, I looked up the hotel, and it had formerly been known, in pre-revolutionary days, as the Hotel Le Royale. Perhaps the right name for this intrigue.

9

The Luxury Hotel was two blocks down on the other side of the street. At the front desk, I asked if there was a Sanders staying there. They looked at their ledger. This was before privacy regulations. I assume they thought I must be Sanders's friend, as foreigners like us always stuck together, of course.

They confirmed a Sanders was in room 702. Yes, they were delighted that Sanders's foreign friend had arrived.

I went upstairs. This was an old building with high, useless, drafty ceilings, with ceiling fans lazily twirling away in the hallways.

I knocked on 702. I could see the point of light in the peephole go dark for a moment, indicating someone looking out. There was a long pause, and then the door opened, revealing Lori standing there.

"Found your brother yet, Sanders?"

She froze, then tilted her head towards me, almost seductively, and slumped against the door frame in an exaggerated display of exasperation.

"Come in," she said, and wheeled around, leading me in.

It was a weird suite of rooms with grand, high ceilings. Three together—a large entry room and living room and bedroom—all in a row. Lori sat down on a sofa in a relaxed way—like someone used to being in a place like this.

"Quite a hotel," I said.

"From a time when it was expected rich foreigners and their families would be staying here for months," she said.

"And what kind of rich foreigner are you?"

Her eyes flashed at me. I sat down across from her very deliberately.

"I just came from a meeting with a... Maurice," I said in a questioning way, to see if she was aware of him.

"You shouldn't get involved with the locals," she said.

"Revolutionaries?" I said.

She laughed a laugh of contempt.

"You are going to end up rotting in jail here if you believe everything you are told," she said. "They are all profiteers here—they don't care about freedom. It's a slogan. They think freedom means no rules, a free-for-all. Just what they want."

The phone rang and she answered.

"Yes, yes. I know... He's here right now," she said with irritation. "He's here now. It's fine." Then adding with sarcasm, "Thanks." She hung up and said to me, "They were supposed to be following you."

"So, you're the dame that got me to come here and lead you to Colm?"

"Yes," she said.

She liked being called a dame. And she was annoyed, but not too much, maybe admiring that I had figured something out.

"All about a crown?" I asked, somewhat loudly, daring to say it out loud. "I'm going to get to the bottom of this just like you want."

She looked at me now really annoyed. Then, after a moment, she decided to confide in me.

"It—the thing—" she emphasized euphemistically, "was never found, as far as we know, after the revolution, but we tried. And others did too. There had been talk that its location must have been known to Colm's father. He was definitely involved as an aide close to many top figures before the revolution. Eyes were on him. Then when he died recently in France, things started to happen.

"There were the reports of fraud from the French Embassy in Bangkok regarding one of his children, Colm. Then a transfer of money by Colm into this country. And we have not been able to find him since he entered here. But the local networks were abuzz. Something was going on. We still don't know what exactly, but we have our suspicions. So, I need to know what you know."

She was being stern and commanding now. "Did he tell you anything? Do you know where he is?"

"No," I said. "I already told you back in Bangkok. He owes me money. And *you* sent *me* here."

"And you knew he had set up a company and where that was," she said. "We didn't know that."

"I guess I was the right man for the job," I said.

"So, tell me. No more secrets," she said. This was police talk to get garrulous wrongdoers to talk their way into jail.

Then she added, "Or things might get dicey for your next visa renewal back in Bangkok."

She nodded at me like a teacher chastising an errant student. That made me mad.

"I really hate when someone doesn't at least dangle a carrot first," I said.

"I don't want anyone to get the wrong idea about what you are up to," she countered. "Do you think you could leave this country if all this comes out?"

"Do you?" I replied.

Silence. She was not used to back talk. She reset.

"It was clever that you knew where his company was here. That's clever. But if you know where Colm is, or where the crown might be, you better start talking now or you won't get much further."

"Okay," I said, standing up abruptly. "I'll just go to the nearest police office and tell them everything I know. What U.S. government department are you with? I can tell your type. Probably working in one of those non-partisan charities filled with spooks?"

She stared at me in a bored way, like she was calling my bluff.

"Wouldn't that solve this situation?" I continued. "The government, if they found the crown, would hide it away and not tell anyone. Maybe they already have it. It's their property anyway."

Lori bristled.

"Okay, okay," she said.

She sighed at me in exasperation.

"Do this for your country—what it stands for in a place like this. Places that do not allow opposition. This is a chance for change."

She watched to see if this boilerplate appeal to my assumed patriotism had worked. Yeah, these government types were very clumsy at doing their jobs.

I shrugged.

"You want me to care?" I said. "What does this mean to me?"

She looked at me disapprovingly.

"We know about you," she said. "Your little foray at the CLB company. Involved with the prime minister over there. We know what happened."

This made me uncomfortable. It was not too long ago that there had been some deaths, unavoidable circumstances, things I had put behind me. There was some subverting of foreign governments, some hurting, well, killing people, also some undeclared money. They could probably get me for that. Yeah, it's always taxes. I had taken a chance and thought I had gotten away with it.[1]

She sensed my momentary concern.

"At least don't say anything to anyone," she said. "Your government needs you. You will be rewarded for information about Colm or the crown, but don't go to the local authorities, okay?"

Then she said sincerely and a bit pleadingly, "Trust me, you could screw us up, and it wouldn't go well for you."

She leaned forward seductively.

"You sure you have nothing more to tell me?" she said.

---

[1] See *In a Country with No Name*, Villefort, 2025

I kept my gaze steady as well as my voice and said as casually as possible, "If I had known anything, I would have told you back in Bangkok."

But I did know more!

In my pocket I had the papers that Colm had tried to keep secret in his desk—with the name "Oungkran Province." I was still a step ahead of her.

Lori was smart, I could tell. She had sent me here and I turned out to be clever enough to uncover something. She took a long look at me again to determine what I might really know. Then she slumped back in the chair, defeated.

"I'm not intriguing enough for you?" she said, mockingly.

She was enjoying this and trying to manipulate me. I played along.

"You are instantly intriguing but become a little bit less so with each minute I am with you," I replied.

She paused, considering how to take this. Then she laughed carelessly and so did I.

She was one of those modern women who men both loathe and desire. And, knowing this, she would laugh a bit in your face.

10

I left the Luxury Hotel, the former Le Royal Hotel, and stepped out onto the dusty street. Even the paved roads in this place were inexplicably dusty. I walked across the street and back to my own hotel.

Now was the time for decisions. I was a young man. I never would be one again. Being here in Asia, even in this backwater, made me feel like I was in the right place in a time of opportunity.

I had been pretty clever so far. And I still had my safe teaching job in Bangkok and the rest of the weekend. If I could find Colm, maybe it would be a big score for me. I had risked more than this before and been lucky. I would be lucky again.

If I didn't try, could I bear to remember the story of when I had a chance to get my stolen money back, but decided not to? I recalled stories like this from friends and relatives when growing up—their greatest tales were of things they had the chance to do or almost did but didn't.

Maybe the money I was cheated of—really through my own foolishness—could be retrieved and this story could be changed from a failure to something achieved.

At that moment, I walked into the cold, bracing air of the lobby of my hotel. It struck me like a bucket of water. And then I spotted her. Deuan was there. Waiting for me. Her eyes locked onto mine.

I walked up to her, and she talked to me through gritted teeth.

"So, are you going? Are you going there?"

This completed my thinking, my next move. I had to make a move while I knew something I was pretty sure Lori did not know. I had to go to the mining concession in Oungkran Province.

I looked around to see if I was going to be rushed again.

"Don't worry. I believe you now," she said.

She took out some papers. They were in the local language and French, neither of which I understood. There were no more than a dozen, some grown brittle with age.

"This is the list of mining concessions from Colm's company," she said. "All small and useless, mined out long ago."

She spread out some half-page letters with stamps and seals, all in the spidery local script.

"These are the rights to plots all over the country. They are letters of concession. They can each be presented to the local governor to allow access to a mining site."

"There's one mine on the list with no letter of access—Mine 18. There are letters for all the others, but not this one. Colm must have taken that letter.

"And I found this." She showed me a letter. "A reply from the military commander in Oungkran Province. It's Mine 18. It can only be accessed through a military base.

"So, he never had enough money to run the company," I said. "That was never the goal. He just wanted access to that mine."

"It says the mine was originally built where a village once stood. That is injustice," she said.

This was a one-party state where government decisions were likely final. It was hard for me to imagine as I traipsed about the world, secure and contented. I nodded to her to show I sympathized.

"Do you know why he wanted Mine 18?" she asked.

"No," I said, but I was lying. Now I was sure that the crown must be there, maybe hidden in the tapped-out mine. Maybe it was something in his late father's effects that alerted Colm to the location. Whatever it was, it was another trail to follow.

I looked at her. The eyes. Neither happy nor sad. Perhaps only determined. That determination bred into people in landlocked countries.

"Can you take me there?" she said. "I'm going too." She grabbed my arm in mock seriousness. She also wanted her money back.

"Is it that obvious I'm going?" I said.

"No, no." I must have been looking at her skeptically, because she added, "Well, yes."

"You think you can do it alone, but you need help," she said. "This is my country. If you don't take me, you'll see me everywhere you go, because I am going also."

There was a resignation about her, like she was used to having to accept the way things were, and this caused her to have indomitable will. It made me believe what she was saying.

"You have no choice," she said. "If not, I'll go to the police. They can't do anything but cause you trouble. And they won't get our money back. I was the office manager and it's my responsibility. To find him."

It was hard enough to do things in a foreign place and this big city, but out in the provinces and getting onto a military base would be another thing. She could guide me, speaking the local language. She had her own reasons to find him. This might work out.

I looked at her and could not tell if she was friend or enemy. She had all the coolness and heat that the most interesting women had.

She looked back at me, probably assessing me as I assessed her. She looked into my eyes, my strangely colored eyes, and I said, "Let's go." I had decided to believe her. I would believe her deep black eyes and imperious manner.

I checked out of my hotel, and we went out the back way through the laundry area and off a small loading dock into an alley of shophouses and restaurants, no doubt catering to the local workers in businesses along the main street.

We moved quickly and I hoped my movements were not apparent to the legions of people who were watching me, still convinced that I would lead them to what we were all seeking.

Getting my money back, or at least besting Colm in some way, was the difference between having a chance at starting my business and having nothing at all, all my own fault. It was the kind of humiliation a young man can feel keenly. It made me desperate.

We got into a taxi and then switched to another one to cover our movements on the way to the airport.

I had no way of knowing if we were getting away with it as we checked into the regional airline. The people here were ciphers to me, and, if I was lucky, I was the same to them—someone one-dimensional and thus clear—some weird stereotype, the strange rich foreigner who is entranced by the heat and the toil and the sweat and the antiquity of the place. An invisible man. A pale foreign adventurer, unaccountably rich compared to them, dull and loud and uncaring. I hoped they thought they could understand me in a moment.

Deuan didn't question any of this, but I felt I had to explain it, so I said, "I am being followed."

She smiled warmly like an old friend and said, "Indeed."

11

Deuan and I were soon waiting in line to board the short flight to Oungkran Province. A man in front of us, a foreigner like me, dropped something.

It fell near my feet, and I picked it up. It was a folder with a "CW Hydro" logo on it. I handed it back to him.

"*Merci*," he said.

Deuan noticed the "CW Hydro" logo and her eyes flashed anger.

"Damming the rivers?" she said, almost like a challenge.

"Yes," he said, mildly.

"Do you know if the people there agree?"

"One of those," the man said to himself.

He was one of those superior French, looking at us through narrowed eyes, a genuine and friendly contemptuousness. One who thought he was more cultured than most people who he met, and probably was. The sort who could be a good friend and yet never drop his innocent superiority.

"All the permits are in place. It is lawful," he said, sincerely trying to explain. "Many of the projects here do not involve reservoirs, you know, just descending tunnels with turbines. It is a blessing of your geography. Where there are people, they are relocated to new houses in towns. It will provide power for the country."

"It's all going over the border," Deuan replied.

"Still, it is a resource for this country," the man said.

"The money goes to the government. And you see how the people live," Deuan said, a bit more loudly.

I gently nudged her. She was speaking too freely for this place with one party, one political line. Anyone in a place like this who thought they were pursuing their own goals without being observed was fooling themselves.

"You don't know who might hear," I whispered to her.

We parted from the man in the hurly burly of boarding the plane. I assumed this French man would not report her, but I was not sure of anyone else.

This was a landlocked nation, a realm of steep hills and mountains. They were unrelenting, and twisted over the landscape, with deep ravines and streams filled with rushing rapids during the rainy season.

It made it a particularly good place for dams to generate electricity, not for this nation, but for neighboring

Thailand, a capitalist giant that thrived in any economic condition and thirsted for electricity for its industry.

We passengers, locals and foreigners, stuffed our bags into the overhead compartments, all single-mindedly focused on the places we had to get to.

Once we were seated, I could still see Deuan's subtle expression of suppressed feeling.

"They are building those hydroelectric projects up in the mountains. All over," Deuan said. "One flooded my grandfather's village. Soldiers arrived and they had to leave their homes. Some people spoke up, and soldiers took away the men, along with my grandfather, to a camp."

She was smoldering in anger again.

"That's how it works. The money goes to the party, and the people must accept it. My uncle took a job working in construction on the hydroelectric project. It's good money," she said wryly.

"And your grandfather?" I said.

"We are waiting for him to be released. We can't speak out. It's different for you from another place. No foreigner could understand this land," she said.

She looked at me, maybe thinking I might be offended.

"I know," I said. "I was just trying to protect you."

"You are very kind," she said. "Perhaps you do not realize how it is when a few put themselves ahead of all others, and one cannot call out in protest."

"I can imagine," I said. "I just want to make sure Colm does not put himself ahead of us."

It was hard to imagine what it would be like to live where a person could not start a new political party or a union or print a newspaper or even read whatever political thought they wanted to. And if the government decided to do something, that was it. There was no room for protest. One had to make sure they got out of the way.

It would hurt a man's heart to knuckle under to all that. There are enough things even in a capitalist nation to humiliate a man, that a man must humble himself to. It would burn for someone like me who had the conceit that he could do whatever he wanted.

"How did you meet Colm?" I asked Deuan.

"I'm the office manager," she said. "Colm hired me. And I hired a dozen others. We leased equipment and worked hard. And then he's gone. He left a note saying he would be back, and we would be paid. 'Be patient.' That's what he said."

"That sounds like him," I said.

"I have my responsibility," she said.

"To who?"

"To the rest of the staff who I hired and who worked in good faith. If I can find him," she said. "I can report him and force the police to take action."

"He may have spent the money already."

"I'm still going to try."

It was the sort of thing I might say.

"And Colm's not that clever, really, I think," she said

I liked that.

"I know he probably only had enough money to do one thing. But why Oungkran Province?" she asked.

I shrugged, playing dumb, but I knew the answer. It was Mine 18, the tapped-out mine—within a military base.

"Sometimes an investor will buy old mines when a new technology arrives that might pry out more gems," she continued. "But people have their eyes on things like this— no assay was made. People wondered what resource he was after—more unfound gems or something else."

She was figuring it out.

"You don't know?" she asked.

"I don't think either of us knows the whole story, although we might think we do," I said.

We both smiled, letting down our charade for a moment. I think we wanted to confide in each other. She was the kind of woman who wanted to make me do that. But we had a mission: get Colm. It was supposed to be about the money after all.

I did not yet know what kind of person Deuan was. I did not know if I was safe with her. Surely, I had misjudged with Colm. But still, she was intriguing, perhaps noble, sometimes remote. This invited me to want to tell her everything and to protect her.

"You appeared at the right time," she said. "And I do think you can find him, for some reason."

"I'm just trying to get my money back from him," I said.

"And I'm just a country girl," she replied.

What must have happened was coming together in my mind. Colm's father, an ally of the old regime, had died, and somehow a clue to the location of the crown had come to light. Colm had found the clue that pointed here.

The money in our account to start the school had been too tempting. Colm had taken it and opened a company, obtaining all its old mining rights. But there was only one site he cared about and that he could afford to manage, so he had abandoned the rest of the company to concentrate on that one mine and what was hidden there.

It was all too much, bigger than I was, all things I barely knew. Yet it made me somehow eager, and hopeful that I would win.

It was a quick flight over sharp mountainous terrain, always weaving, with deep vales, receding into mist. This was a land of impenetrable clay, a land that resisted attempts to put it to use, yet farms were everywhere, cut into the steep slopes. Hard men and women made these steep terraces, pounded from the soil. And now, above all, monumental power cable towers were being erected over the mountains.

"If Colm is out there, we will find him," I told Deuan.

I looked down at the land we flew over. Every place that could be planted was sectioned off, every inch squeezed and plucked of its fecundity, every grain of rice collected.

"It is hard to imagine anything is left to be found," she said.

I was beginning to have sympathy for the men on their red clay hills. But it seemed that nothing could change in this place. How can one seethe for years in such circumstances? Seethe and accept the humiliation of things you cannot change? I felt bad to realize that such trials were beyond me, the privileged man who bestrode nations, riding in this plane with its sleek alien architecture.

12

When we arrived in Oungkran Province, I had to sign in at a police desk at the airport, as did all foreigners who traveled from province to province in this nation. I guess we needed to be kept track of, but the police officer sitting at the weathered old desk did not even look up at me.

We exited the terminal—it was a warehouse-like building, little more than a metal pole-barn, erected so the passengers would not get rained on while waiting.

I looked around, trying to determine who might be watching us. So many people seeing me and no one looking at me. I guess I was the center of my world, but not anyone else's.

We got into a taxi, a late-model American car with a badly cracked windshield. The driver, a smooth-faced older man with sharp cheekbones and a good haircut, tried to engage us in conversation.

"What country?"

"U.S.," I said.

"Oh!" He was thrilled. "On holiday?"

"Yeah, a bit. I work in Bangkok."

"How often do you go back home to your country?"

"Not too often," I said. I liked being away.

"My daughter has a house in Orange County," he said. "I visit every year."

"That's a nice area," I said.

This was a standard exchange for any foreigner like me with a local who knew my language: Where are you from? Then mentioning their own connection to my country.

After their war, many refugees from this part of the world ended up purchasing homes in California, especially Orange County. This was something I could never do in these jealous countries, jealous of giving away any of their sacred land to a foreigner. Yet, they came to my land and bought a house in Orange County and put their daughters through high school and university, daughters who would turn out to be disapproving of their father and his corruption and mistresses.

The driver pulled out a laminated sheet and handed it to me.

"I have a certificate from Texas," he said.

It was a "Summer Certification Program in Biology" from the University of Texas, Austin.

I wondered what he would need with such knowledge, but I knew many nations like this were filled with the over-educated, sometimes with multiple degrees, who ended up driving taxis in places that made no truck for the employment advancement of their people.

He was smiling proudly like I was his old friend and would be interested to know of him and his accomplishments.

I was, somehow.

I was surprised that it touched me so much. We all have our hopes and plans. I hoped he would find success.

He looked back and saw me trying to work out his name on the certificate. His name was like a Thai's name, long and multi-syllabled, full of meaning I could not understand.

"Call me Johnny," he said brightly.

He did not look like a "Johnny." He was older, graying hair, but still, the aura of his peak manhood was not too far out of sight. I could imagine him smoking a cigarette, musing about his choice of work now that it was too late to change anything.

"Hope you have a good holiday," he said.

He had a subtle hint of cockiness to him, like he had sized me up and judged I was wanting—yet he was driving me around in his country for pennies.

We went through a police checkpoint exiting the airport and headed on to the military base—to the address I had for the mining concession office.

The road wound between steep hills that were almost becoming mountains.

We passed by a farm where the land rose right up from the roadside. High up, a young man, certainly a teenager, was toiling away. Below, near the road, was a thatched shack where a young woman held a baby in a sling around her neck. She looked up the hill towards her husband. The red and orange of the upturned earth suggested meager harvests. We drove on.

Then there appeared on the road tiny red cloth bundles with green leaves sticking out. One here, one there, in the road.

Deuan said, "Rice seedlings. Someone dropped them."

"Very precious," added Johnny. "Very bad luck."

We came upon a girl on a motorcycle driving back in our direction. She had an oversize box on the back of the motorcycle filled with the green rice seedlings.

She was stopping to pick up the tiny seedlings that had fallen from her motorcycle. She had that blank haunted expectant look, like only endless days of hard work awaited.

I noticed Deuan watching her with a solemn reverence. Then Deuan noticed that I was noticing her, and I caught the sense of her feeling for this place. This world will break your heart.

We passed by the girl on the motorcycle collecting her dropped rice seedlings. But as she had her labors, I had mine. I was going to find Colm and get back my money.

We came up to a military checkpoint at the entrance to the military base. Deuan spoke to the men there. They were suspicious of me but pointed us down the road.

"They said the mining company has an office up the road," she said. "And yes, another pale foreigner was there, just this morning."

We exchanged glances. Colm!

The taxi approached a row of shophouses in front of a steep hillside. These were offices and small businesses that no doubt served the base.

The driver pointed to one of the shophouses. It was the address we were looking for—the local address of Colm's business.

The building was gloriously aflame, the flames matching the deep red of the clay mud on the street. Deuan and I got out of the taxi, studying the scene in disbelief.

Each level of the three-story building was engulfed. A pickup truck was there with men moving about and spraying water from a small nozzle mounted on the back of the truck. Large canisters of chemical spray were being wheeled into place. A makeshift ladder, welded together from what looked like strips of cast-off metal, was taken off a truck and placed on the ground in case it was needed.

The men had faded uniforms and flip flops. They scurried around performing all of the tasks that a fire required. But it was just activity—both a valiant effort and entirely futile. There was no saving this building. It was gutted.

"What was our plan anyway?" Deuan asked me.

"We thought Colm would be here. This is the office address."

"What if he was?"

"Well, I guess we would have demanded our money back."

It sounded dumb to say it. It was a peculiar dead end.

She looked me over. I had the feeling she was wondering if I could be any help to her—or to anyone.

The wind blew the smell of smoke towards us, and the flames flew up, illuminating the hills behind the building. It was elemental destruction, the items in the building being converted to smoke and ash and ascending up and away on this hot afternoon.

Maybe I should inform Lori, whoever she was. But if everyone was following me, she would know I was here and would know of the burning office. And did I really think Colm could pay me back? He was using the money for something.

So, the way was closed.

I looked over and saw the golden light play upon Deuan's face. At least I was here in this strange place, on this strange weekend, with her.

She looked back at me. I tried to look hopeful and not confused.

We turned back to the car, where Johnny eyed the fire as if he were entertained and it would make a great story when he got home to his family that night, a break in an otherwise uniform working day.

"Ah," he said, offhandedly. "Bad luck, eh?"

Usually, the locals out here, even the surliest of taxi drivers, were polite, almost courtly. And this would be the case, just like back in Thailand, even after they were insulted—the mask stays on. But Johnny's flippant response was unusual. I thought he was probably trying to be friendly and casual, maybe like a glib American, mocking me in a friendly way.

"Yeah, bad luck," I said.

"So, where to?" he said.

I looked to Deuan. She said nothing.

"I guess into town," I said.

We got in and headed back the way we had come.

"Gonna start a café in town," Johnny said as we drove along. "I will have more than one salary! I'm going to call it 'Johnny's.' Good to have dreams, right?"

"Yeah," I said.

It was funny to have a much older man ask for approval from me, by virtue that I was seen as a valuable Western tourist, but that is how the world was.

"How many businesses do you have?" he asked.

"Uh. None." I said.

Johnny looked surprised. Maybe he assumed that everyone in capitalist countries who had a chance to make their fortune would do so.

My mind was back to considering myself the fool. I had sort of expected finding Colm to be easy. It was odd that I often thought like this when I knew everything was hard.

Johnny began smoking one of the cheap, foul-smelling cigarettes on sale everywhere here.

"Smoke?" he said.

"No, thanks, I don't smoke," I said.

He gave me a thumbs-up. I saw him looking at me and then Deuan in the rear-view mirror. A kindly look came over his face.

"If I were a man who could do anything, go anywhere," he said. "You know what I would do?"

"No," I said.

"I would appreciate it," he said.

It was strangely friendly advice, and it made me think of how little I had accomplished in my life.

We were driven into a small town. It consisted of three parallel roads with hardly any traffic. Along the road were clustered shoulder-to-shoulder concrete shophouses. Beyond them were scattered warehouses and residences ringed by high cement walls. The whole town was squeezed together as though space was a priority, but just a few meters from where the town ended was empty land and rice fields and beyond that, the jutting hills that covered most of the land.

We alighted at a tiny traffic circle in the center of town. A bare, cracked concrete mound stood in the center of the circle and a line of taxis waited along the road.

"A monument was here in the olden days. It was taken away," Johnny said, like he was a tour guide. He looked at us, watching what we might say in reply. Neither of us said anything. I paid him, and he drove away.

"It was a monument from before the revolution," Deuan said, as if further explaining what the taxi driver could not. "Its history was erased."

I stood there, distractedly, hands on hips, thinking of my next move and considering writing a letter of complaint to the universe.

"So, how can we find Colm now?" I asked.

"I don't know," said Deuan. "It seems someone doesn't like his business. What do you think he was doing out there?"

"Don't you know?" I said.

"No. Do you?" she said.

I paused, maybe a bit too long, maybe letting on there was more I would not ever say to her. She looked back at me, somehow both innocently and knowingly.

There was suddenly little reason to be together, yet it still felt good to be here with her. Something in her eyes for a moment betrayed that she was feeling the same way. It buoyed my spirits.

We walked along the street, one like any other, a street of meager businesses, old concrete buildings, pressed together as buildings tended to be on remote streets in Southeast Asia.

Tiny festive lights were hung here and there around a few restaurants and bars. It was the Festival of the Golden

Moon, or something like that, and many people were in town. Something about Buddhism.

When I first got out here from the West, I dutifully read up on every cultural thing I should have known, but now I was a bit jaded. I probably knew as much about their festivals as the locals did when enjoying Christmas in my country. Something about Santa and Jesus on the cross.

What the festival meant to me now was that there were no hotel rooms available.

Deuan asked a shop owner if he knew of a place to stay, and we were directed down an alleyway in between buildings—a roadway too small for full-sized vehicles, but with businesses and shops tucked into every available spot.

Alleyways like this were as valid for travel as roads, so we found ourselves leaping out of the way for motorcycles roaring along with gas canisters for cooking or bundles of goods being delivered to businesses.

The alleyway suddenly opened up to reveal a wooden mansion, a proud structure from the past. Its owners had developed its once green lawns into commercial shophouses until finally the old family home was imprisoned by the buildings surrounding it. Its roof was patched with tarps, its inhabitants having long since lost the inclination to repair it. Squatters then moved in, and innumerable naked children wandered about, scowling, their hair askew. The squatters operated small food carts. Clusters of these carts nearly blocked the pathways in every direction, imprisoning the old wooden house.

We passed by and into another narrow alley and then came upon a shrine entrance, a locked gate with police officers standing in front. A group of people holding votive objects—candles and incense sticks—were standing in line waiting for it to be unlocked.

Deuan explained. "It is the city shrine temple—locked up by the government. They will soon unlock it for the festival."

I noticed she was seething again when saying this.

"Milady," a man said to her in greeting. She gave a little nod in response.

"They have no choice but to unlock it on the holy day, the day of our land," she explained. "There will be crowds tomorrow morning, the traditional time to pray. The government downplays it but cannot stop it. They do not like the beliefs of the people."

13

We gave up looking for a hotel for the moment and decided to eat at an open-air restaurant.

It was a festive place, with little holiday lights twinkling all around. A few foreign men, Westerners like me, and their local wives or girlfriends were seated there.

We went to the bar while waiting for a table. A red-faced white man was seated at the bar and turned to me. He was clearly looking for someone to talk to. You know the type.

"I'm Pete. American?" he asked.

He could probably tell from looking at me.

"I'm from Utah," he continued. "Where you from?"

"From California. On holiday," I said.

I usually never told these types who I really was or where I was from. A lot of them were desperate. Like I was.

It was clear who Pete was, and I saw it—the bottle on the table, a glass with amber liquid, and condensated water from the side of the bottle pooling on the table.

Deuan sat watching us with no expression, strange foreign creatures in her land, just seeing us, noticing things that were, I guess.

"I used to work for the CIA," Pete said.

These types were everywhere out here—the guy who says he was once in the CIA—often a jolly, slightly paunchy American who grinned a lot and paused after he revealed it to see if you were impressed.

Maybe it was something he once had said to impress the local girls, but then a switch was flipped and he had to tell everyone—right away. He was a nobody, fleeing from his nothingness, here, in the remotest place, pretending he was somebody.

I gave him a perfunctory nod, but he knew I was not impressed.

"Nice to be here for the festival," I said, just to say something. Deuan watched. She probably thought that this was what our type was like—sweaty, dissolute, drinking every afternoon.

"What are you doing here? Oh yeah, holiday," Pete said. "I'm with Tegakari... Trucking."

He sighed, no doubt ready to divulge the trials and tribulations of his business life in the harsh sun.

"Poor place to have to be stationed," he said. "Don't know why they sent me here or why I agreed to go. Nothing out here."

"Yeah," I said. I looked around for the waitress, hoping our table was ready.

"I thought I was going somewhere and I was... to nowhere!" He laughed to himself. "Buy you a drink?"

"No thanks. I'm waiting for a table," I said, looking at his drink.

"Sure. There's nothing here. What little there was was drowned by the dams," he said, rambling. "The country makes the money—the company makes the money—not someone like us. We're too late."

I did not like that idea. He was looking at the bottle, and I thought I should say something, tell him he was wrong, but he continued.

"This place made me pray," he said. "They made me pray. I'm not who I used to be, but it's still me. I deserve a chance, don't I? I should never have come out here, done so many things. They never stop following..."

Probably something to do with spirits, I thought, looking at the row of bottles behind the bar.

He smiled at me, coming out of his fog for a moment, a bit embarrassed, perhaps.

"What's there to do?" he asked.

"I... I don't know," I said. "Impossible to know."

"Or not necessary," he said and laughed the clear laugh of a drunken man.

Our table was ready, and I escaped the conversation.

"That guy," I said to Deuan.

"Yeah, lots of them out here," she said.

"We are not all like that," I said, as a large beer glass was sat down for me.

I pushed back my drink, resolving again to stop. Or probably to cut back. Then I took a drink. Tomorrow.

"I never asked you before, what is your business in Bangkok?" she asked.

Her question was the sort of thing one might answer with, "I was once in the CIA." Something to make myself feel bigger and better.

I was a teacher, but I did not want to say that. I knew teaching was highly revered out here, but it seemed to me the work of a drudge. It certainly was not what I aspired to. And yet it hit me that I did not know what I really wanted yet. I was casting about with big business schemes, wanting to do something impressive, wanting to get in on the prosperity all around me.

"Trying to make a fortune," I replied. "But I was working at a school as a teacher."

I was surprised I admitted it to her. It was clear, I guess, that I was a nobody, risking everything on crazy schemes with little chance of success. A man with Quixotic plans.

"I'm not just a teacher," I told her. "I was working at a media company last year, not in Thailand, but in another country, and there was some political instability."

I did not want to explain to Deuan exactly my involvement.

"I heard about that. There was some fighting," she said.

"I had to leave quickly," I said. "I came back to teach in Bangkok again. But I teamed up with Colm and another guy and we were going to start a school."

"You sound like one of my countrymen," she said. "In a nation like mine—a socialist one—where it is hardest to get ahead, one finds the most rapacious capitalists."

"Despite the government's best efforts?" I said.

"No," she replied. "They know it happens and sometimes encourage it. This system hollows out morality, the common impulse for kindness. Then, all that is left is the party."

"Makes me feel that my need for success is tainted," I said.

She looked at me like a hawk, her head tipped forward a tiny bit, regarding me, weighing me.

"We are all tainted here. There's no other way. You are pure in the way you are tainted. Your obsession for success, business, even drink."

Women say the truest things and men must accept it.

"Time can pass quickly in a place like this," she said.

I nodded to mean, "I know."

Yes, I was stuck in the heat of empty feelings and blurred time, just like the easy-going locals. I was becoming one of them.

I found myself holding up the glass of beer and looking at it.

We ate the local fare. It was some type of curry, I think. It was hot and unusual and thrillingly natural to my Western senses. Every part of the food tasted like it had come right off the land from some special plant known by local experience to provide that particular zing of taste. There was not a hint of something processed, like I was used to and usually preferred.

Deuan was amused at my liking of her culture's food.

"It is the food of the poor," she said.

14

A waitress gave us directions to a hotel deep in the warren of alleys we had walked through earlier.

We finally found the tiny hotel, a series of dorm-like workers' rooms. This would do for the night. I was glad Deuan was here because I would never have found the place without her.

We got two rooms, "one for the lady and one for the gentleman," befitting the morals of the rural workers coming to reside there, no doubt.

There was always relief after finding a hotel. I then knew where I would be, at least for the night.

After checking in, I found my eyes meeting hers—her luminous black eyes and my dry sharp ones—and within was all the intrigue that could result.

I suddenly felt the need for propriety. There was something different about her and I did not want her to think I desired conquest or had mindless flings.

The sound of fireworks called us to the festival outside and we decided to take a walk in the twilight. Outside on the main street, people were milling around, buying food from the many carts set up for the festival.

Some crazy kids were lighting small firecrackers and throwing them at each other, jumping out of the way at the last moment, marvelously lucky to escape the scalding heat every time. My ears were soon ringing from the sharp retorts as we passed by.

With hills and mountains all around, evening came quickly.

"We don't really see the sunset here. Only the moon," Deuan said.

This sweltering land was the land of the moon.

I considered my money. I was surprised at how the thought of losing, of being bested by Colm, could still reach me on a night like this. I wasn't sure if my sense of self held me back or was the thing that pushed me forward. Maybe both.

At least I was here with her, in the cool air under the full moon.

I found her hand on my elbow, as if to support me. I touched her hand for a moment, there on the eve of this festival, and that was all that was needed. We walked on and held hands after a while.

"I did not think I would be here, on this auspicious day, with a foreigner like you," she said.

Yet she regarded me with affection, I could tell. We were starting to understand each other in the way you do sometimes when you are suddenly faced with an intriguing person.

"I don't know our next move, or anything really, but it's okay," I said.

It was a rare admission for me, to relax, to accept myself, my failures, and the joy of it all.

"Yes. It's okay," she said.

I studied her face again, as knowable or unknowable as any other human face, really. Yes, at some point we have to decide that what we know about another is enough—that it is all we are going to get.

Music was being played over a loudspeaker in the street. It was a song sung in an old scratchy, high-pitched voice coming to us over the decades, from another time.

"An old recording of a hymn of the holiday," she said. "A girl forever reaches out to embrace the precious moon. She wants to keep it for herself."

Some children walked past us, singing along with the song.

"It is a remembrance of times past, when our traditions were not a crime," she explained.

We walked under the moon and its sky, past men in a field shooting into the sky at the moon.

"A tradition of the festival?" I asked.

"To frighten the spirits," she said. "And call for the moon."

She said something about men and the moon, reaching out to become one with the sky, the sheltering sky overhead.

It was one of those evenings, those nights, that we walked, without intent, without program, without agenda or decision. We walked abroad on this festival night as two walking together can, knowing that someday we would remember this night, on some future day when we might be long parted.

We returned to our hotel, an unfamiliar place made familiar by the tone of the day, this holiday, and the girl, the lady who was by my side.

We did not wish to part on this night, and we did not. We held one another and our dreams throughout the night, even after the boys stopped throwing their firecrackers at each other.

15

It was Saturday, finally the weekend, and the sun was strong in the morning.

We had not spoken about our next move. Our mission of finding Colm and getting our money back had faded during the otherworldly night of the festival and Deuan's mysterious eyes.

Silently, we ventured out onto the street. We walked down the alleys, already bustling with the old women who had been up since dawn, buying foodstuffs and setting up their food carts for the day.

We walked along and pondered the strange curries, piles of silvery fish with rich brown flesh, black crabs with sharp shells, and shards of fatty cooked pork hanging in the sun. And chilies—always chilies—pounded into a mush that made everything spicy and bright and bracing.

Deuan was still cool and intriguing as we sat down and ordered food. She was proud and still remote somehow.

"Do you have brothers or sisters?" I asked her.

"No," she said. "The line is dying out."

"Only you?" I said.

"I am not important," she said.

I could sense the depths of her feelings, so I placed my hand on hers for a moment.

"Do you have siblings?" she asked me.

"Yes. Three brothers," I said.

"And you are the oldest?"

"Yes. You can tell?"

"Yes. The burden of making something of yourself," she said.

I was quiet for a moment. I had grown up seeing the end of industry in my own land. Men were well-paid factory workers one day and delivering newspapers the next. I did not ever want to be humiliated like that.

I noticed Deuan regarding me, judging who I was and what I was thinking.

"I'm happy we met," I said.

"As am I," she replied.

It was all we needed to say in the moment.

Somehow, unexpected things happen. Being alive one morning on Earth and seeing this enigmatic girl looking at me.

Then, from somewhere back out on the main street, a loudspeaker blared out an announcement.

Deuan became alert and listened.

"What is it?" I asked.

"Searching for someone," she said.

She grabbed my hand and led me to a radio that was playing in one of the businesses that fronted the alley. It was all talk in the local gibberish and then my name, "Bert Mars." Deuan went rigid.

"You are being sought," she said. "They wish to speak with the foreigner who was sighted there. For involvement with the fire. Another foreigner died in the fire. They found his passport—it was Colm."

"Colm?" I said in amazement. "And they are looking for me?"

Something had gone wrong. The gears had been turning against me while I slept.

I thought to myself, "I'm never getting my money back."

Colm was gone and I was here, witnessing it. Someone I knew had to die over this. It was who I had trusted and who had cheated me and who I was happy to go into business with. Who, like me, thought everything would work out fine. First his father passed and now he had, and over some strange scheme. It was a situation I thought I was too smart to become involved in—yet I was involved in it.

We ducked into a doorway as uniformed men walked down the alley.

"Those are military," Deuan said. "They will be searching all the hotels for you."

"People have seen you," she continued. "You have to get out of town and out of the country. It does not matter that I was with you the entire time. The authorities never look for the wrong person. You understand? It's gonna be you."

We made our way out to the main street and walked along, somewhat briskly, trying to appear calm. Our eyes met a few times.

"Colm wasn't as clever as I thought," Deuan said.

"I'm not as clever as I thought either," I said.

I had had my revenge on Colm, at least. A friend and an enemy dead. I would consider it all later, when I knew I would be chastened by the tragedy of it all, but for now, it seemed fate was having its revenge on me, making me a wanted man.

The military men were moving along, some way behind us, looking into shops and scanning the street. This was not good.

A car pulled up beside us.

"Tourists walking in the sun," the driver said. It was said with a lilting fatalism. It was Maurice.

"Fancy a ride?" he asked.

"Your friend?" Deuan said.

"A lot of people were looking for Colm," I said.

"Someone apparently found him," Maurice said.

I wanted to protest his accusation, but the men moving down the street were getting closer. The street here was otherwise empty, lined with cement block walls and fences. Nowhere to hide. We looked at each other. There was no choice. We got into the car.

"Milady," Maurice said to Deuan, and the car pulled away.

"Following me?" I asked him in a friendly manner.

"I told you before, we can find you. We are watching," Maurice said.

Then he said to me, "I can see you are a resourceful young man. I suspected as much. My employer would very much like to meet you. It's nearby. And safe."

Deuan and I exchanged glances.

"Sure," I said. We had no better option.

We soon arrived at a small compound, a cement home, nestled alongside many others, where the more wealthy of the town lived, all cloistered behind dark windows and high walls. A "for rent" sign was posted on the entrance gate.

Gates closed behind us as we drove in. Instead of feeling menace, there was relief. We were hidden for now at least.

The entry hall of the home had a gaudy chandelier hanging overhead and a shiny wooden floor. It was crisply air-conditioned but smelled a bit musty. A beam of heavy sunlight shone through a skylight overhead and bits of dust rose in the air. It was like all these houses in the tropics—a pocket of climate only just resisting the harshness of the greater world.

Someone was moving in. Boxes of antiques were being unpacked. Old household implements, farming tools, vases and knickknacks were being placed on shelves.

"My employer travels with his collection," Maurice said. "He likes to be surrounded by the past."

He showed Deuan to a sofa.

"You may wait here, Milady," Maurice said. "You need not be troubled further. We will return presently."

"Thank you," she said.

I followed Maurice through the house to a room with tinted windows looking out onto a spectacular view—rice fields with sharp mountains in the background. An air conditioner chugged away loudly right outside the window. From inside, in the cool air and through the tinted windows, the view looked idyllic and inviting.

Before the window was seated a strange scowling local—perhaps half European. He looked as satisfied as a scowling man could be. I think the scowl was his version of a smile.

He was surrounded by antiques on small tables and cabinets. One cabinet had rows of intriguing tiny drawers. Old books were lined up on a table. A large oval rug lay on the floor, decorated with the designs of far-off lands, and faded with wear.

It was the bric-a-brac of the past and in a coarse concrete room of the present.

The man looked at me pleasantly, then returned to his scowl. He was smoking cigarettes like he was attacking them.

"Hello, sir," he said. "I would appreciate it if we could have a few words."

He gestured for me to sit down.

"He was alone?" the man asked Maurice.

"With a local. She knows nothing," Maurice answered.

The man paused for a moment, considering.

"Very well. Pour the boy a drink," he said to Maurice.

He was waiting for me to say something. Instead, I sat down and remained silent. Something in his heavily lidded eyes, the dark circles around his face, said to me that he was someone who could get the job done and thus should be applauded or feared.

After a moment, he said dramatically, "I am a collector. One of the few left who still relishes history."

He motioned at the antiques around him with pride.

"I am... well, you may call me the Keeper. Maurice has told you of me?"

He spoke like a fat man, but he was not too fat except for an exaggerated belly. A belly that was static and content and that was taking over.

Maurice had not mentioned him before, but I said, "Yes."

Maurice looked pleased.

"Hmmm, yes," the Keeper said, studying me. Then he leaned forward in an almost friendly way.

"I am always willing to be lucky," he said. "Willing to take a chance in this world that tells me not to, that says I can't get ahead. That says everything is getting worse."

Maurice then asked me quietly, "What will you have?"

I said, "Gin tonic. Make it a double."

The Keeper noted this interruption in his speech but continued.

"I search for things that can rarely be found, that are foolish to even search for. It is a noble pursuit... I believe," he said as if acceding it was only his own opinion. "I have traveled here to Oungkran Province because everyone is here, as you must know... following you."

"You, in my country, on the trail of the greatest prize of all." He leaned forward and his stomach moved with him like it was another person trying to keep up.

I could feel his innocent and pure greed. I imagined that, if he had the crown, he would immediately try it on, maybe sleep in it—whatever he could do to possess it and hold it close to him.

"You are clever," the Keeper said. "Knowing to somehow come to this city."

I shrugged.

"There's no reason to hold anything back now, I guess," I said. "It was Mine 18 on the mountainside on land behind the military base, the only concession that Colm cared about. No person could go poking around there with bulldozers without owning the company and thus the rights to mining the land."

"How did Colm know to search there?"

"I don't know exactly. His father had recently died back in France. Something must have come up in his father's estate, his papers, but it's something that I don't know. Whatever Colm found, it triggered all this."

Maurice handed me a glass and I took a drink.

The Keeper leaned forward a bit. "And you, he owes you money?"

"He stole from me," I replied. "We were going to start a business back in Bangkok and he used the money for the concession he needed to control here."

The Keeper leaned back. "Well, it doesn't matter now, I suppose. You made neat work of it."

"Colm? The fire? That wasn't me," I said. "For all I know, you did it."

"Yes, DARVO. Always science from you Americans," the Keeper said to himself like he already knew me inside out.

"We didn't peg you for a murderer," Maurice said to me with a devilish grin. "You seemed too gentle."

I did not want to appear as a murderer, but I took it as an insult that they did not think I was capable of it.

"Look, what are you guys after?" I said. "I don't know how to get the crown. It's probably on the concession behind the base. We all know that. And now someone has set me up for what happened to Colm."

"Have you been in contact with any other parties?" the Keeper said.

"Seems everyone knows what I'm doing and where I go, even the government, maybe," I said.

Maurice added accusingly, "You have met with the lady? Ms. Lori?"

"The imperialist," the Keeper chortled.

I nodded.

"She's probably around here somewhere, managing your revolution," I said, seeing if this talk would faze him.

"We are not yet at the edge of revolution," the Keeper said. "Some of my countrymen have dreams of it. Rubbish! The land and its people are sleepy, our villages remote, the land sparsely populated, the past regime already forgotten by most. There is not a hint of unease. There is no chance now. The land is in a contended oppression. Revolution is out of our grasp."

"Not everyone feels the same way," I said. "But I'll take your word for it."

The Keeper waved his hand as if to silence me.

"I have not accomplished all I have by being a fool," he said. "I suspect that you know precisely more than you are letting on. You would not have come to this far province if you did not know more than you have told us."

I did not know how to argue this. I had no doubt that, besides these guys, Lori, and maybe others, were watching. They all thought I had some special knowledge about Colm. And perhaps I did.

Maybe the Keeper saw the wheels turning in my head because he immediately responded.

"Don't worry, I will keep you safe, my dear boy. You will be rewarded for your information," he said. "But you should know that I will do anything to win."

I replied, "So will I."

He was beginning to annoy me.

"You just want to put history in a drawer," I said. "Possess it. I understand you."

"I understand you also," he said. "A young man, flailing at things you want, things that always slip through your fingers. And I do know what history is. I know I cannot collect yearning, desire, ambition. Only the thing. If you think you can do more, you are the fool."

The Keeper chuckled to himself.

"I have no illusions about history," he said. "Only the delusions of my hobby."

He pondered for a moment.

"So, very well," he said. "I will know what you know."

This was said in both a friendly and odious way and I believed him. I still had the paperwork from Colm's office in my pocket. Maybe I could give him that, but that would only prove I had been holding back information. I had fled from one danger into another here and brought Deuan along.

I stood up uncomfortably. I realized I needed to get away from these men. The Keeper was a hoarder of things and now I was to be one of them. I backed casually towards the door I had entered from.

Two burly local men entered from the other side of the room as though suddenly summoned to detain me.

"Sit down, my boy. I understand," the Keeper said, cautioning me from a risky action. "You wanted your money back, or else. Your own ambition is showing."

"There is no escape for you out there," Maurice added. "The authorities are nothing if not relentless."

This was a moment of manly terror. I was not going to give in. We were all poised, waiting for the other to make a move.

I stood there, confronting the men. Challenging the universe. Willing to be lucky. Calculating how I would get away and rescue Deuan as well.

Then I snapped to alertness, as, at my side, there was the sound of a gun being cocked.

"Let's go," Deuan said commandingly.

She was at my side, with a shotgun trained on them.

"Milady," Maurice said, in protest.

The Keeper's composure did not crack. He looked over to the men.

"Idiots," he said. "How did you let her get at the guns?"

Then to Deuan, he said, "That is a valuable gun, and it will shoot. But do not make things worse by firing it."

Deuan held steady. The way she was aiming gave me the sense she would not miss, and it would hurt.

"Look, my dear boy," the Keeper said to me. "I understand if you do not want our protection, but I cannot let you leave here knowing what you know. And I know your type; you do know more than you are letting on."

"You are a good judge of character," I said.

"So," the Keeper said. "Are you going to stay here, out of reach of those who are seeking you now?"

It was an offer, for sure. A chance, to not escape, but to be held by these types to some unknown end.

"I'll take my chances. I always have."

Deuan and I backed away as the two men advanced on us. I picked up a chair and tossed it in their direction.

"Now, there's no need for that," Maurice said.

The men came closer. I motioned to Deuan not to fire. We started moving out the door Deuan had entered through.

Then, someone on the other side of the door closed the door with Deuan on that side of it, leaving me alone to fight the two men.

I am not much of a fighter, but I have fought before. I know what can happen. I had felt the terror of grappling for my life. Thus, I knew I had to go all out, to hurt, with no concern for myself.

I moved fast. I kicked one away, pushed the other, then tussled with the first one again, grasping his collar and holding him while punching him repeatedly. This worked well but was as painful for my hand as I am sure it was for his face. That kind of punching makes one aware of what a human is—soft flesh over cracking stone.

I pushed the man back into the other thug, who was approaching again as I stumbled a bit.

Suddenly, there was a great gunshot sound from behind the door. It was a compact ringing followed by a sudden silence.

We all paused. The door swung open. The feet of a man were visible. Deuan was standing over him defiantly, having just shot him. Her hair was disheveled, yet she looked otherwise unfazed.

She pulled me through the door, and I shut and locked it behind me. The man was groaning on the floor. I could not see where he was hit, but he was contorted in pain.

"You shot him," I said.

"He had to be shot," she said, a bit surprised she was saying it.

Yes, we were all business. She tossed the shotgun onto a settee as if it were suddenly too hot to hold.

"My grandfather taught me to shoot. I don't miss," she said.

I saw her, capable from head to foot, as she smoothed her hair back into place.

"I believe you," I said, trying not to let my voice tremble.

I had been involved with violence in the past, and it was only in the remembering of it, in the echo of it, that made me shake at the reality of the taking of lives and how close I had been to it.

For now, it was just a little moment, and then we were running, exiting the compound and out into the street.

All the houses had high cement walls and gates in front. There were no sidewalks. The street was empty, with just the sunlight bouncing off the concrete.

We ran down the street. There were several ways to go, and we had almost turned a corner out of sight of the house when I saw Maurice stepping out from the compound and clearly spotting us.

A moment later, two men emerged, and Maurice directed them in the opposite direction from where we were.

We hurried away in our escape.

Soon, a car pulled alongside us and the window rolled down. It was Maurice again.

"My employer is often... audacious," Maurice said. "You must understand, as I suspect someone like you knows, there are compromises that have to be made. Ones that we are not always proud of. I sincerely apologize."

There was gentle hurt in his eyes.

He leaned towards me and said, "It is revolution. That is my hidden goal. I tell you this because I know you have your own hidden goals."

"Fine," I said. "Now we both have enough information to doom the other."

Maurice nodded and continued. "Maybe it's time for you to go back home. Whether you were... vengeful or not, your appearance at the scene of the fire was well-documented. You would not like our prisons here. Dirty."

"Point taken," I said. "Thanks for looking the other way back there and letting us get away."

Maurice nodded, clearly pleased.

"Um, I would not trust anyone," he said. "I'm going to fetch a doctor."

He nodded at us both and drove off.

"That guy back there must not be too badly hurt," I said. "Maurice doesn't seem to be in a hurry."

"Don't believe him," Deuan said. "They would say anything. They are profiteers. There are always those in my country."

Still, I was hoping that man was not dead. We did not need any more trouble.

16

We emerged onto a larger street of shops and commercial buildings. There were uniformed men who seemed to be going from store to store up the street. I would soon be found if they were looking for me. Deuan and I hid behind a half wall in front of a closed shop.

"I have to get out of this town and back to Thailand," I said.

I knew it and she knew it, but it was an admission, a concession to the present I could not change.

"Wait here," she said. "I'll get a motorcycle."

I sat down, making sure I was out of sight of the street. I was breathing heavily. Fully alert. I peeked out over the wall. There were more soldiers in a truck driving by.

I must not get caught. I could not turn myself in. Could I really say that I knew nothing? And now Deuan had shot someone, maybe killed them. It crossed my mind how easy it would be to blame everything on me, the hapless foreigner. I could be in custody for months, maybe years, trying to deny it. I could not lie well and there was no guessing what a good interrogator would be able to get out of me with time.

I crouched back behind the wall as uniformed men passed by. This was getting serious.

Without warning, someone reached over the wall. A man grabbed me by the arm and wrenched me up. A car sped up to the curb. I swung at the man and missed, as another man came around the wall, grabbing my other arm. I could not pull away. I was bigger, but they were lean and conditioned and used to the hot sun.

They propelled me across the sidewalk and into the waiting car.

The door slammed and the car sped off so fast that I was pressed against the back seat. I tried to open the door, but it was locked—one of those electric locks taxis had in these countries.

There was a partition separating me from the driver. I frantically pounded on it, but the driver, a brutish-looking man, ignored me.

I tried to open the door again but was repeatedly thrown off balance as the car careened from street to street. The town was small, so I realized I would soon know where I was being taken.

The car skidded to a stop and the door unlocked automatically as I was pushing it as hard as I could. I fell out of the car and hard onto the road.

I looked up. I was at the closed gate of a Buddhist temple at the end of a quiet street at the edge of the town. A dog that was wandering about stopped to look at me quizzically.

"Temple of the Golden Moon" was in small English letters on the temple gate under the name of the place in the local language.

Deuan glided up on a motorcycle with a sidecar filled with coconuts. She looked like a local girl taking things to market.

"I had to improvise to get you out of town quickly," she said. "Everyone is on the lookout for you. Just stay at this temple for tonight. I'll find us a way to get back to the capital. You can't fly. And there are checkpoints on the roads now."

The driver gave her a little salute and a mocking laugh for me as he drove off.

I got up, brushing myself off, not wanting to show I had panicked.

"Thanks," I said. "I couldn't have done any of this without you."

"I know," she said. She was a good girl under fire.

The gate to the temple grounds opened a bit, as though someone was cautiously opening it, inviting me inside.

"You'll blend in here," she said. "I'll be back tomorrow. Don't worry, you'll get away."

I must have looked worried. I was not so sure I could get away this time.

We neared each other and I wanted to kiss her, for how she was saving me, for us in this time, but I was not sure such a thing was done here, even on this empty dead-end street.

She then grabbed my shirt, almost an involuntary movement, and we kissed, just for an instant.

Before I could speak, Deuan roared off in a cloud of dust and I was alone in the late-afternoon sun.

I turned towards the temple. The gate was still open a bit, beckoning me. I slipped through.

Inside was a varied collection of temple buildings, white with high-pitched roofs. A cat slinked here and there.

A robed monk, a young man, appeared pushing the gate closed behind me. He gestured me onwards.

I walked towards an area with a few trees, a courtyard in between buildings. I began to notice foreigners—my kind—seated about, not in monk's attire, but in light blue hospital-style garb, heads bowed.

One was shaking, one stood motionless. Most were still, human statues, looking, or even glaring into nothingness. One was being patted on the back as he vomited into a bucket.

I felt a hand on my arm. I turned to see a lean young Westerner with an old face, smiling through his grief and wear.

"It's okay, brother," he said. "This is a good place. You can set down your burden here."

I must have looked confused, because he added, "You'll learn. They'll dry you out."

Then I realized. This was an addicts' temple, where the derelicts of European nations came for a drying out from their fun of drug and alcohol abuse.

"I'm Ian, mate," he said, shaking my hand enthusiastically. I could see his mind was enthusiastic, but his body was not—he was sweating profusely and—I could feel it through his handshake—he was shaking. A tremor.

I looked around at the suffering men. Sweating it out. No psychological therapy. No one telling them that they had not been loved enough. No assertions that addicts have no control. That was the Western way.

This was a fat camp for drug and alcohol addiction to simply dry people out with a brutal regimen of temple life in the sun. For many, it was a last resort after their own culture's conception of addiction and how it should be treated had failed to cure them.

I could see a guy heaving into a bucket nearby, next to what looked like a latrine. Another was frantically drinking from a large bottle of water. Others were under a sala, seated cross-legged, sweating in the slanting light of the day—and they were all smiling—maybe because it did not matter if one smiled or frowned. So, they smiled. This is what the world can do to us—or rather, what we did to ourselves.

"What's your thing?" Ian said. "Drink?"

I nodded yes, blankly. Maybe he could tell.

I was unsatisfied with my ambition sometimes. I was unsure if I could really make something out of myself. And look where I was now—with my fellow addicts. I was not sure if I was disheartened that I had ended up here or maybe I was lucky.

Another young man, eager to get in on the conversation with the newcomer, said, "Me too. I was locked up twice for drunk driving. And even that didn't stop me. That's how I ended up here. It's working."

He said it almost like a question and then laughed a mirthless laugh.

He was young but already had the sad eyes of a rummy, with red around the edges, so that when he looked in the mirror, it must have told him what he was doing to himself.

"We all need help," Ian continued. "We all want peace. You can have it too."

This was the welcome for me. I was just another lost foreigner arriving to sign up for the program. They assumed I had made my way to the right place.

I was seated in the courtyard as other men appeared and sat down as well. A monk arrived and gave me a bottle of water and a small, reddish pill.

"Herbal," he said. "It will help."

I chewed the pill and drank the cool water.

The pill tasted like the incense sticks that were burned in temples—thick, old, and pungent. I had seen and tasted such things in Thailand. It contained both a fresh, sharp taste and a deep, velvety dusty taste.

I do not know if such things worked, but somehow the taste made me feel that something was moving through me, disinfecting and cleaning.

Someone screamed out, as if in reply to what I was thinking, screaming for the chemicals their brains were trained to desire. How did I end up here? It was a mystery, but a mystery that I knew the answer to.

I could see the types here—withered young men, older reprobates, former tough guys laid low by chemicals—all having to use their finite store of attention and ambition to manage their self-created demons.

I sat there, strangely contented finally, drinking water in the precincts of the temple, occasionally noting the moving limbs of the trees overhead. Finally, I was not thinking of anything.

It was late afternoon by then. A monk stepped onto a long platform in the courtyard and picked up a wireless microphone—the kind from a karaoke machine. He was placid and elderly, someone who never moved quickly. I could tell he was the head monk—the abbot. There was fluidity and gravity in him that proved that the speed at which he moved was the correct one. His appearance somehow indicated that peace was present. This caused the frazzled men before him to let their attention be drawn to his words.

The abbot spoke into the crackling microphone. "You are far away from most anything that can touch you: the old stories of your lives, the temptations, but you are here to return to yourself."

I didn't know the truth of this, but it was getting to me. Addiction always starts with supreme confidence that a person is having the best fun. It ends with the abject opposite of that. I was a fool for letting myself become like this—that I now was even considering that I was one of them.

I wondered what would have happened if I had not become involved with Colm's schemes and, instead, had stuck with my plans to lease the land at the beach. I should be there on the beach now.

But, no, I was here, entangled. I was bound up in saving face, just like the local Thai men we foreign teachers at the school used to sneer at—the men who would never allow themselves to be slighted and would go down in ruins to assuage their hurt egos.

I was all the way out here in this mountainous place—tricked into it, apparently, by Lori. And a hunted man. And not an hour before, I had been in a house where a man had been shot.

Things that could happen were beginning to pile up. I doubted there could be any secrets in the world for long. Things get told. Things want to be told. I guess this story itself is something like that.

I had to rationalize it. Maybe these were the right kind of problems to have. These were problems that occurred because I was trying to do something. I had nothing, but was taking a chance. I was here, and here there was a chance.

I was kneeling with the others, thinking this and sweating and listening to the abbot.

My body had been formed to sit in chairs. Maybe just those few dozen generations since the beginning of the age of chairs had done this—selected my genes for chairs instead of kneeling. Whatever it was, my knees were screaming as the tendons stretched, but the others were calmly seated, not shifting as I was, maybe feeling some peace.

Something inside me yearned, roared for something, alcohol for sure, that hunger beyond hunger, but also something else. I was trying now, trying hard, risking a lot, maybe for no good reason. Probably to my own detriment again.

Not long ago, in another nearby nation, I had tried to make my fortune and had colluded with rich men to overthrow other rich men. I had taken up arms and taken a chance, and I had done things which I now regretted. It was in the service of my goals and unavoidable—things that had happened in the moment. It was hard to live with that.

And now, scary things were happening again. Maybe if they caught me and pinned Colm's death on me, it would be okay. I deserved it, if not for Colm, but for other things. Maybe I could live with that.

The abbot was saying something about the moon and men like us spontaneously arriving here to hear these words, as the first monks did during the full moon, in the legendary past.

"Yes! It is the eve of this festival—of the full moon—and we were all here," he explained.

"The need for release—from food, drunkenness, fear of decrepitude," he said, "is as close to the elementals of life as yearnings for love and life and immortality."

It was all a bit disjointed, some Eastern wisdom being distilled into English and then into my Western mind, but, still, I relaxed hearing those words. Yesterday and tomorrow were flowing away, flowing back to the moment right now, glowing and sparkling.

The abbot concluded with, "All efforts to become must cease."

Ian spoke to me hopefully, "Do you believe it?"

I involuntarily chuckled at him. That shocked me, as it was a chortle of my contemptuous feeling towards belief— the sort of scoffing anti-religious attitude I had been fed by my culture all of my life.

"Don't laugh, brother. You can do it," Ian said, with all the sincerity in the world.

I was suddenly emotional. Maybe I was one of them.

I placed my hand on the little red amulet, the tiny Buddhist image I wore as a necklace.

It was a belief that cleared the mind and helped me to not suffer so much when I had to do difficult things in an uncertain time.

You can keep your anxiety pills and neuroses. Perhaps it is better to just believe in the magic behind the world. It made sense being here with all these addicts on this festival eve.

Ian was still waiting for my answer.

"Yes. I believe it," I said.

And I did believe it, and here I was, with hale, hearty men, all as foolish as me.

I could hear the background noise of my world now, the rushing of blood in my ears. A low whoosh I would always hear as long as I lived. It was part of the physical world, my body, my vehicle, the vehicle I had ruined, changing the chemistry of my brain to create an everlasting hunger.

17

Ian lifted me up from where I had slumped forward onto my forehead. I had fainted.

The speech was over, and no one was taking any particular notice of me.

"Hey, man," Ian said. "Don't worry, this happens all the time."

He opened a bottle of water and pressed it to my mouth.

"Too much sun maybe," I said after a long swig.

"You'll get over it," he said. "I did."

He was so earnest, it hurt me. Ian had ceased to be a monkey man like me and wanted some real meaning.

"Abbot needs to see you now. Check you out." And then to reassure me. "It's the same for everyone. Then you'll be seen by the doc."

He patted me on the shoulder. "Brother, it's okay. We are all on the same path. And the way is known."

It was so convincing that, for a moment, I could remember my full life again, what it really should be about, and it almost made me tear up.

"Thanks, brother," I replied.

I was shown to the main temple building, a whitewashed cement building with a pitched red roof. I was directed to go inside.

I walked alone through the dim interior. There was a still, thick air in such places and I could smell incense sticks and dampness. The waning light fell against one wall where mystical and exaggerated men and creatures were painted in a flowing mural. Such creatures were portrayed with a flat perspective, as though our realm could not properly perceive the divine.

There was always a large golden Buddha at the head of such a temple, but I could not see it in the darkness.

At the far end of the room was the outline of a door. I entered and walked unsteadily down a dim hall. I felt foolish to have passed out. I think my brain had rebelled, trying to tell me something I was not ready to hear.

A light shone from beneath the door I was approaching. I pushed it open.

Beyond was a large rectangular room—clearly the office of the abbot. There was a large desk as well as a table on one side of the room covered with piles of papers, stacked in peaceful abandon.

On the far side of the room was a shrine with Buddhist images as well as local totems of luck, and animist images mixed with Buddhism. Behind it was a wall of what looked like government documents.

The abbot was suddenly beside me. I had not seen anyone else in the room, nor any other doors. Maybe I was still woozy.

Close up, he seemed ancient, but somehow spry, a child peeking out from behind wrinkles.

Before I could speak, he began. "You arrived here at the temple without prior summons at this time—the moon festival—as did the 1250 enlightened monks who arrived to hear the Buddha."

He looked at me warmly, to assure me, a supposedly skeptical Westerner, that this was his belief.

Maybe this was a speech the abbot gave to everyone— an introductory pep talk.

"The way to this place," he said, "is not apparent. It is to grasp and not to grasp. So, to arrive at this time, it is a sign—a sign of the age."

So, if this monk, here under a golden moon, on this festival day, believed that I was meant to be here, guided here through all the eons of time, I was more than willing to believe him. In the remaining fog of my recent faint, I was already believing him, while not entirely understanding.

"We have been waiting," he continued.

He stopped and looked at me, really looked at me, studying my face again.

"We have been waiting. Your father was a great man. Faithful," he said.

I realized my mouth was open in surprise and slowly closed it. So, he thought I was Colm. Maybe he had not heard the news of the fire.

"Your return here after your father's death was closely watched. There are many who wish for the diadem to appear. For a new day to dawn." And then, with real emotion, he said, "And you arrived here, on this day of all days."

His message to me was profound, all right, but for the wrong person. Maybe I was close enough.

"I have long been... nothing but a bureaucrat." The abbot gestured at an array of permits and documents on the wall. "Permits and regulations, every month, to keep operating.

"Perhaps it is easiest to co-opt religion like this—regulate it, tax it," he said. "Always forms to fill out."

"It is how they tire us," he continued. "And I am tired. At my age, maybe it is time to be taking this last step."

"This last step?" I said.

"I was... I am," he corrected himself, "Loyal to the old regime." He stopped for a moment as if he expected the authorities to rush in and arrest him. The moment passed and his admission invigorated him.

"The precious royalty and the lives of the men... common farmers..." the abbot continued. "Too much has been lost. There is too much greed. Too much sin. The breaking down of men. This is the day of fulfillment. As the last courtiers said, before they disappeared forever into the camps, 'It will be given to the right person.'"

I recalled the writing on the photo of the estate I had: "Oungkran Province, see the gold moon—it will be given to the right person."

I felt close to the truth of what was really happening.

A young monk entered. The abbot put his finger to his lips to indicate for me not to say anything. The monk handed the abbot an old-style cigar box and left the room.

The abbot opened it and inside were many papers. Among the papers was a folded newspaper article. The abbot unfolded it and silently showed me. It was the same newspaper clipping as I had taken from Colm's office—the crown and its pale blue sapphire—the "Moon Gemstone."

Next, he showed me a map. An old map of the area. Badly folded and mangled.

He took out a ballpoint pen. The ink was almost gone. He scratched a dot on the map. Then he handed me the map and said, "What we seek is still in reach. Even I do not know exactly where it is, but it is within this province. Your father's company mined this land, long ago, in the old times."

He gestured at the mark he had made on the map.

I looked at it. I instantly saw that he had marked a spot on the land within the present-day military base, the site of the mine Colm had attempted to search. I tried not to look disappointed. It was a place I could never reach now, not after the fire. But the abbot had a look of hope.

"It may not be possible," I said meekly.

"No, it is time. The word is already spreading throughout the network about your return... that you are here and on this holy day. Things can only happen now."

It was tempting to come clean and tell him who I really was—that I was an adventurer, who had hurt people, killed people in the past and regretted it. But I was deep into the lie that I was Colm and probably should not muddy the waters by admitting my sins.

I swallowed my revelations like men often have to do to get by. They would have to wait for another day.

"I can tell," the abbot said, almost ethereally, "that you are indeed meant to be here."

I felt dizzy again and staggered a bit.

"I haven't had anything to eat... or drink," I said.

"A man cannot live on hunger; there must be a sating," the abbot said.

"I'm all hunger these days," I replied.

He laughed at this with detachment—with the true detachment of his belief.

It seemed that there was some question I needed to ask, some wisdom still to be gained, but the young monk poked his head in the door and spoke urgently. I could not understand him, but I could tell it was a message of alarm.

"Army men, not police," the abbot said to me, dropping his serene manner. "You cannot stay here now. There is nothing more this bureaucrat can do."

The young monk spoke to him again.

Looking to me, the abbot said, "He will show you the way out."

"Thank you. Goodbye," I said, placing the map he had given me in my pocket.

As I left, I could see the hopefulness in his eyes. I was sad that I was not who he thought I was. I again considered telling him the truth, but I allowed the urgency of the situation to push me on.

I was forever on my way, here, there, trying to be something.

The young monk showed me out the back way of the temple grounds onto a trail that led up the hillside into a forest.

The moon was now rising over the hill, made gold by the black-green of the earth below it, far away as a rare coin found on the beach and as close as a piercing porch light.

Glimpsing the moon then, it was like the first time—a strange thing that announced there were worlds beyond and I was a little thing below it, clinging to the earth like the farmers clinging to the hills.

The young monk said something to me in his language, in an overly expressive way, in the way we think there is something commonsensical about our own tongue, and just by speaking emphatically and loudly, any other human will understand.

I guessed it was something about how far it was back to town perhaps. I couldn't understand it, but I had to go on. I had no choice. I hurried down the trail from the temple and into a dark forest.

18

The trail led me through a shallow valley and over a hill that skirted the edge of the temple. I looked back and saw the men in the temple walking along in a candle-lit procession in the twilight, no doubt something to do with the festival.

I was sorry to leave my addict brothers and their struggle, their sweat and vomit, and hopefulness. Man and his efforts.

The candles were moving along, circling the main temple building, trembling in the hands of the men in the gathering night. I hoped I might visit them again someday, but, no, I never would.

I rushed away, and then I was alone. Trees soared above me and vines hung down in anticipation. I carefully stepped over the roots that should have tripped me. I walked quickly and quietly, urgently moving away, always away.

I heard the occasional cawing animal. These were thick, pure sounds that rang out and then drifted away. One was a bird sound, I think, like a train on tracks clacking away, a creature I did not know the name of, and neither did it know nor care of me.

I came to a fork in the trail. One direction was a bit brighter than the other, so I chose that. The worst that could happen would be I would have to go back. Such was life.

The path led to a forested hillock. I walked under the canopy of trees that covered the hilltop and came to a jumble of huge black stones. They were vessels, large legendary jars of some past culture. They were overturned, agitated, as time does to the works of men. The jars lay scattered in every orientation, with pale green lichen covering them.

They were empty now, their stories forgotten, just as mine would surely be someday. This made me feel better. I breathed in the cool air.

Beyond the hill were pits, a few meters deep. These were bomb craters of a more recent war, gifts from my own land to a nation caught in between the fortunes of greater powers.

When I was young, I had learned about the Vietnam War, and the details of my country's baffling misadventures in Southeast Asia. I understood the intended lessons—how bad war and the United States were.

I had read of the fall of capitals, Saigon and later Phnom Penh—and of the end of the niceties of society that we all assume exist automatically.

But when I had read of this, I could not help but think, "That sounds like fun."

I knew that conflict was a tragedy, but I was thrilled by events bigger than I was. I wanted to be a part of it, or at least a witness to the momentary void in civilization. I could live by my wits. I would create my own legend.

Such were the things a hunted young man considers while fleeing through a forest at night.

The trees swayed, reaching out into the last of the blue sky of that day, and beyond that, my eye caught sight of the moon again, oddly high in the still-blue sky, bold and patterned, waiting for the dark to catch up with it. I knew it would be there, brighter and bolder by the hour, and I could watch it and hope.

It was all too much, really. What I wanted was all quite physical—money and accomplishments, maybe some fame, and I was realizing, a little alarmingly, that I was lumping alcohol on top of all of that. I realized this because I was not a barbarian fool. I knew facts and science, so I knew that, bit by bit, the ranking of alcohol was moving up the chain of necessities for me, replacing everything else. Perhaps someday to even replace the elemental desire to stay alive.

The world was turning, ever moving, and I was on the arc of it, the hint of a breeze coming with the shadows.

I walked off the path and found a rippling stream, strange to find on the top of a hill. It must have been welling up from a spring somewhere.

Kneeling before it, I pondered what pollutants man in his urge for progress had put there. But I was thirsty again, almost woozy and trembling in my dryness. There were a million reasons not to drink from the stream, yet I did not think I could go on without water.

The water was cold, with the empty taste pure water has, and yet it had an immediately satisfying and bewitching effect.

The water helped steel me. Risk was everywhere, and I resolved to eat it up, despite having lost my money and now maybe my freedom to Colm.

I knew I was a stereotype walking down dusty streets, no different than Ian back at the temple, or drunken Pete. I was a Roman tourist in Luxor in ancient times—there by virtue of my relative wealth—or maybe just a fly that got caught in the car and then was let out hundreds of miles away.

I found a mossy mound in the crook of the twisted roots of a huge tree. I sat down to rest for a moment. I could feel the hardness in the soles of my feet, and the machinery of my legs slightly sore.

"All efforts to become must cease."

The abbot's words rang in my head. Could I live without the things that I thought I wanted? Who was I without my ambition?

I felt in my pocket for the map he had given me. It was both full of hope and useless. I felt for the necklace that held the red amulet of my forsaken girlfriend. I gripped it, squeezing out a salve for my uncertainty.

Despite my predicament, I still thought that I was the right person, appearing at the right time. I had put myself here and made things happen, walking through a strange forest.

No one seemed to be following me. I was getting away. The spirits that followed Pete back at the bar could not follow me here.

I could feel sleepiness coming. It was in my skull, my brain telling me this was too much, that I should sleep. I leaned back. The hill all around was still, overgrown, primordial.

At some point my eyes closed, and I slept as bugs swirled. I was the furthest away that I had ever been.

The leaves of the trees made unknown shapes overhead. I dreamed of being in a white room—waiting to be judged by others.

Then a high note, like a tiny flute, came from somewhere in the forest, maybe nearby or far off, a strange, rare animal that knew man and avoided him.

And the dream was over. Mosquitoes roused me. I was back in the physical world. Its mosquitoes could not allow me to rest for long.

I continued onward. The night air was beginning to move, cool and thick, soothing me. And the moon was nearly full, strangely large, peeking at me over the treetops.

There was a fine line between adventure and disaster. It was time to get away. In this tiny country, I could get on a plane and be back to Thailand in no time. I would have to swallow my pride and ambition and live with the sense of loose ends. I would not get my money back. This would be a story of escaping disaster at the last moment. It would not be the first time or the last.

Some bright object flew by overhead. It was low, a silent thing, just above the treetops. I could follow its glow as it moved away. Aliens over the forest maybe. There were many strange things that I will never know.

Throughout the night, I walked. I was probably lost and there were mysteries all around, but I was enjoying it. A bit.

I finally emerged from the forest onto flat lands. These were all sectioned into rice fields. Across the fields, I saw the town I had fled from. The moon lit up the land like midday as I walked between the water-filled rice fields on the raised mounds of land between them. The rice plants had a green vividness that glowed in the moonlight.

I would find Deuan again somehow. Hopefully, she would have arranged some way for me to get back to the capital. And I missed her.

I weaved my way back and forth through the fields towards the lights of the town in the distance. Soon, I came to a foot bridge—really just planks over a deep chasm—the kind that might be a rushing torrent during the rainy season. I had to step carefully so as not to stumble into the blackness below.

At the end of the foot bridge was the beginning of the outskirts of town, a few houses and shuttered buildings pressed up against a quiet street.

I had almost escaped. Just had to find Deuan. It felt odd to be so concerned about someone I had only known for a few days, but she had become special to me in that short time.

As I stepped off the bridge, uniformed men emerged from the bushes. Men with guns in green uniforms. Guns at the ready.

There was uncertainty in their stance—ready to shoot, but fearful of me.

I was too tired to resist. They noticed my hesitation. I was immediately seized upon from all around. They had finally gotten me.

19

I had an unexpectedly deep sleep. The still hot air of the jail cell held me snugly. It was the air of resignation. I studied the pattern of the chipped paint on the wall until I fell asleep. Maybe for once I was sure of where I was and what was going to happen. I was secure finally, perhaps permanently removed from concerns about what I was going to do and my glorious future.

Still, I had to wake up. It was still dark, but I could hear roosters crowing in the distance. Other prisoners were seated around the cell, passively looking at me. All characters, each seemingly carved out of dark sandalwood, smooth and shiny and inert, all as resigned to their fate as I was.

Being arrested in a foreign land is strange. On one hand, there is hope—most of these nations are not strictly law and order. There is always a chance for bribery or just mercy, and thus some expectation that even the most heinous of crimes might be overlooked.

On the other hand, the longer it goes on, the more the fear rises of being asked to sign unintelligible foreign-language documents and then slowly slumping into the maul of a backward, barbaric system. And I knew enough of these countries to realize that a foreigner deemed undesirable could be lumbered by torturous legal cases and threats of long, unreasonable sentences. This was done to shut him up and grind him down. Both Lori and Maurice had warned me of this.

Before dawn, we were all called out into a common area and given food. It was rice and strips of fish with some sauce. It was delicious, but I suspected this was a poor-man's meal—the cheapest thing they could serve to the lowliest men.

The other prisoners were glaring at me as I ate. I think this is what one was supposed to do in jail: size up the newcomer.

A lean man with huge eyes was sitting next to me. The whites of his eyes stood out as he peered at me.

"What happened?" he asked kindly.

"I am sure they will let me know soon," I said, trying to appear confused by my predicament.

"You been here long?" I asked him.

"Some time, I guess," he said. "Not up to me."

"I was selling," he said. "And the undercover man came to get me."

I understood he meant that he had been selling drugs. Yeah, he had that look.

He grabbed my arm.

"Gotta watch out for undercover men. So many," he said. "Things happen, I guess."

His entire face looked at me contentedly. He had big wet Indian eyes that I thought would never look jaded, but always innocent and accepting, whether free or in jail.

"Charhadi," he said, meaning that was his name.

"I'm Bert," I said, and we shook hands in a Western manner.

"I thought your kind were always lucky," he said, sincerely.

"I guess not," I said.

"Perhaps your fate is to be here," he said thoughtfully.

He was on someone else's train through the world. I knew people like this, even in my own land, who would never connect anything they did with any outcome. It was all the luck of the draw, or some unknowable random will of a higher power.

Charhadi had a certain kind of serenity. Perhaps that would be the kind of feeling I would have to embrace if I was stuck here for long.

I was realizing then that they had me in with the common druggies. That was never good in these countries where penalties for such offences are severe. They were giving no special treatment for the Westerner.

I pondered what I would say in reply to their questions.

"I'm just a tourist."

That made me instantly understandable. It made my motives shallow. My actions careless and innocent. Yes, I was just a tourist.

A tiny warder walked up, looked me in the eye and gestured to me to follow him. The urge to panic was rising.

Charhadi gave me a nod as I left. It was a nod of absolute pleasantness, his head cocked in some placid bemusement, his mind apparently not fretting on any past slight or ambition.

How strange to be a person who did not realize they were the author of their own disasters.

The warder led me down a couple of long hallways and into an office. I sat on a wooden chair in a waiting area—no shackles, no bars on the windows.

It was a room of desks with police bureaucrats slowly working away. Each looked up once and regarded me, expressionless, and then returned to their endless tasks.

The walls were lined with tall cabinets, with shelves inside holding bundles of paperwork. Name a country in Southeast Asia—this will be exactly the style of officialdom of bureaucracy, police, immigration, and trade. Identical wooden desks and cabinets, forms, stamps and deliberately moving people, permanently hunched over paperwork, slowly checking, stamping, writing. Bureaucracy was the cure for everything.

The clock was ticking. The time for intervention—a phone call from a savior—was receding as more people knew about the foreigner caught in the web. I was imagining someone excitedly telling his boss he had caught an American.

I had to decide how to handle this—frantically or with peace. Accepting or fighting it. I recalled the advice given to me by a comrade on a previous adventure when we were both being held captive. He had said, "I know my doom, it sits on my head smiling."

It was something from his culture, something he said before going into battle, and thinking of that made me resolve that they were not going to see me crack. I would not wither under the circumstances I had found myself in. I would smile and be grateful for my plight.

A lone police officer, a sleepy looking man, came over to me. He motioned to me to get up. He kept his expression remote. I was beginning to feel insulted. I was not shackled in any way. No one thought I was dangerous at all.

I was already thinking I should demand to speak to my nation's consulate. I looked at this man guiding me. I assumed he did not speak my language, and if he did, he could not help me. Side by side, we looked like different species—I was an angular, lumbering figure in my rumpled clothes, and he a miniature, tightly-packed brown figure in a crisp uniform, moving along with small steps and a certain air of efficiency.

We left the jail building, a dim, crumbling hulk. I instantly felt the thrill of the cool air on my skin and the terror of being incarcerated. This was serious.

I was led over to another building. It was a new concrete structure, bright white in the morning sun. This building appeared to be offices and facilities for the higher-ups in police here.

The man did not enter but showed me through the door. This building was as bright as the jail building was dim. Once inside, it was bracingly cold. It was the way the locals liked it if they could get it—frigid air conditioning, as if to make up for millennia where their ancestors had toiled in the unrelenting sun.

A lady at a desk pointed me to a door. This was the entrance to a conference room.

I entered and approached a large table in a brilliantly white room with shiny white floor tiles, and white walls and ceiling. This was the bureaucratic tone of the region— that of a higher level, to impress with newness and sleekness, unlike the disordered world outside.

A man stood on the other side of the table—a local— with an uncertain look on his face. He motioned for me to sit down. His expression never changed as I looked at him, expecting him to speak.

I waited. The man remained standing while watching me. Someone outside was cutting vines growing over the windows. I noticed mold growing near an air conditioner vent on the wall.

After a moment, I could tell this man standing at the table was waiting for the person who was actually in charge.

I heard vehicles arriving outside. The man looked back as if to make sure the person he was expecting was really arriving.

For some reason, I thought that the Keeper would appear or at least Maurice—Maurice seemed to be shadowing my every move.

The man turned back to me, stood up straight and said the words he had practiced and was ready to say ever since I had arrived: "Your American consular."

A door opened and a woman walked in. It was Lori.

She gestured to the local man to leave. He scurried out of the room, his expression never changing.

She had a smart business dress on, no doubt exotic foreign attire to the locals. Her shapely angular legs shone in the fluorescent light of the room. I was sure that she liked to dazzle the local men she met in the course of her duties, who were not used to this style of dress.

She cocked her head and smiled at me. I think she saw my mouth open in surprise.

"Out of things to say, Mars?"

"Yep," I said.

She tossed a passport onto the table so it slid over to me.

"You really made a mess of it," she said.

"It wasn't me," I said. "I didn't kill anyone."

Her bureaucrat's demeanor was almost seductive, perhaps deciding what I was capable of.

"Like I said, it's a mess," she snarled.

"So, what about Colm? What about the charges?"

"All sorted out. All under control," she said. The way she said it made me feel dumb for asking.

I opened the passport, looking at the passport photo. Yes, it was mine and this was really happening.

"What's going to happen to the old mine up there?" I said.

"Just leave," she sighed. "Here's a plane ticket. You should not have any trouble getting out of the country."

She slid a ticket sleeve across the table to me. I silently examined it. It was to first fly me back from here to the capital and then return me to Thailand.

After a moment, she offered, "You're welcome. You are off the hook, but only for now. It's easy for foreigners to end up in jail here on drug charges—especially those who get in the way of things they couldn't possibly understand."

I wanted to say something back, cool and snarky, but I couldn't. She was enjoying this and I was almost trembling with relief.

On one side of the room was a long black window which I happened to notice then—perhaps a one-way mirror with people watching on the other side.

"It's complicated now," she said, in a friendly, advising tone. It seemed she was tired of being tough with me. "Just leave."

"Glad to see my country is looking out for me," I said.

"Your country is aware of you," she replied.

We looked at each other in silence, expressionless. It gave me a chance to realize that now I was two or three steps behind her. And she knew it.

"Go," she said and gestured to the door.

It was humiliating, but I was a foreigner partaking of the unbelievable boon of luck in the tropics. I was getting away.

"Nice to see the real you, at least," I said as I got up.

"You too," she said.

I stood there, looking rumpled, hair uncombed after a night in the forest and a jail cell, and grasping my travel documents—the paperwork that made me a being worthy of travel between lands.

I had no further clever thing to say, so I shuffled out of the room.

A crummy old taxi was outside waiting for me, and a few police officers watched me with interest, as if making sure I would leave quickly. Lori had had the last word.

20

I was dropped back on the main road in town, near the
bus stop for the bus to the airport. But I was not ready to go
just yet.

I followed the alleyways again between the buildings
where I had walked with Deuan when we first arrived here.
That seemed like a long time ago, but it was still the same
weekend, a long holiday weekend, the sort when the world
pauses for a time, and I had found myself in this town, and
in a temple, and in a forest, and in a jail cell, and now
searching for a singular girl.

The Keeper might find me, his men might be searching, but I needed to find Deuan.

My steps passed the restaurant where I had met Pete at the bar, and then passed the old wooden mansion, enclosed by modern concrete buildings.

At first, I did not know where I was going, but my feet were leading me somewhere.

And then I knew where.

I began to sense, then smell, the incense. A hot, dusty, otherworldly smell. An infusing, enclosing smell that drew me to the city shrine on this holy day—the shrine entrance Deuan and I had passed the day before, now unlocked with adherents going in and out.

The shrine itself was a red-roofed wooden building, penned in between modern cement structures stained with black lichen.

A gong was being struck inside, and people clogged the entrance. I slowly worked my way into the shrine through the crowds.

Inside were arcane images clustered all around, and rituals, strange to me, comforting to the initiated. Much of it was recognizable as motifs imported by the Chinese diaspora. They were part of the culture of the region, intermeshed with local religion in a system that was welcoming rather than exclusionary of foreign beliefs.

Another typical feature of such places: the floors were clean, but cobwebs caked with incense dust covered everything else, giving a strange ancientness yet lived-in quality to the place. I suppressed a sneeze, not wanting to make any discordant sound.

Statues, golden idols, and wooden figures peered out at me: A withered hermit. A frolicking lion. A serious monk. Smiling faces, fierce faces. A wide-eyed dragon, mouth open in relish.

It was a warren of spaces, each room randomly added, bit by bit, without overall planning, creating darkness with bright gold and always the thickness of incense.

One could study and delineate, in scientific terms, what all this was. One could go to school and learn the context and influences of the beliefs... all information that few of the adherents here would know or care about.

I could have learned about it, separating it from the vital belief, so that I could never feel it, unlike the kneeling old woman here before me, praying with eyes tightly shut.

A wrinkled man passed by with lit incense, and a bit of the hot ash wafted onto my arm, burning me a bit. The man looked at me in a moment of terror, then pity for me, his head trembling in an attempt to express that he was sorry.

I tried to put an expression on my face that showed no harm was done. He started to reach out to pat my arm, but decided not to and ventured on, into the depths of the temple.

So, I would forever be on the outside. Maybe, I could not be a true believer anywhere.

I expected to see the Keeper and his goons, Maurice and his secret sympathies, maybe Lori, maybe the ghost of Colm emerging out of the darkness to find me and apologize.

But I was looking for her in a haze of incense.

She was lost, the only thing that shouldn't be lost.

And then, as if waking from the desperation of a dream, I saw her. Deuan was there, kneeling and praying, surrounded by other adherents.

Before her were photos sitting on easels. One photo showed a fetching woman with a conservative hairdo, wearing a wraparound gown. The other photo was of a man. It looked like a university yearbook photo. He looked both noble and uncomfortable. Both photos showed people looking into our time from a past age. They looked to me like the photos of royals in the twentieth century—wary, as though carefully considering their roles, if not their very lives, as the world heaved around them.

I sat down with the kneeling people, taking in the surroundings, imagining what it would be like if these signs and symbols had meaning for me. And knowing I was here with all the people who needed them on this festival day.

Relaxing into the moment, into myself, I watched Deuan praying. It made me feel sad that my culture had worked so hard to teach me that belief was stupid and useless. And that I had listened. It had taken something from me, some peace I did not think I could have anymore.

I pondered this until the incense began to sting my eyes and my knees ached again.

At that moment, Deuan finished her prayer and got up. I struggled to my feet—not being used to standing up from a kneeling position.

Our eyes then met in a shared expression of surprise and happiness.

"I found you," I said.

"I prayed on this day for blessings on you," she said. "And I wondered where you were."

"Maybe your prayers saved me," I said. I sort of believed it.

"I was concerned when the abbot said you had to flee again," she said.

"They got me finally, but now I'm free—free to go at least. It's a long story."

"You do have friends in high places. More than you know, perhaps," she said.

"I believe it," I said. "I'm not in trouble, at least for now, but I wanted to find you."

She looked at me and took my hand and we started to make our way out of the temple.

"Those photos?" I said, referring to the photos on easels. "The old regime?"

"Only on this day," she said. "They could not stop the photos being displayed. The people would not stand for it. And then they go back, hidden away. Bringing them out is a small compromise to the people."

It made me realize all the big things going on in this land while I was just having an adventure, passing through.

People parted as we exited the shrine, with a group of men greeting her with "Milady."

"They know you?" I asked.

"No, I'm just a country girl."

We walked down the alley together in silence, happy to have found one another again. We emerged from the alley and entered the restaurant we had been to the day before. It was empty except for good old Pete, sitting at the same place at the end of the bar.

"I thought today was a holiday," I said to him. "A holy day. The moon festival? No alcohol?"

"We find a way," Pete said.

A waitress brought him a coffee cup.

"It's the local rotgut served under the table," he said. "It's okay. I'm not one of them. The police don't care."

Still, he drank it furtively.

He was a memorable guy, doing better than when we met the first time, but still probably beyond help. Deuan looked on sedately, with the slightest hint of disapproval.

I must have been looking at the cup greedily, because Pete said, "You don't want it."

"Yeah. I know," I said solemnly.

"I can't have too much either," he said. "Sending some new trucks out today—even though it's a holiday. Must be important."

Deuan and I exchanged glances.

"Out to where?" I asked.

Pete was not paying attention to me. He drained the mug and then turned it upside down on the table.

"Just taking a break. Got to get back to the office."

He struggled to his feet.

"Wait, running trucks out where?" I said.

"To the base," he said, putting on a wide-brimmed hat that made him look like a nineteenth-century tourist.

"Where? The military base?" I asked.

"Yeah," he said. "There's nothing out there. It's tapped out, but still they dig. Hey, as long as they pay for the trucks."

He walked out of the restaurant and across the road to a building with a sign that read "Tegakari." A line of vehicles—dump trucks and a couple flatbeds with backhoes—were in an adjacent yard.

"Could it be?" Deuan said. "Someone is still digging out there?"

"Someone..." I said.

We walked out to the streetside. A line of gleaming yellow and orange trucks was leaving the yard, raising dust which occasionally swept into our faces.

A truck came by and stopped in front of us, so that a lowly horse-drawn cart could enter the road from an adjoining street.

Maybe it was the heat or my fatigue or maybe my ambition to make this work out in my favor, but I leapt up on the running board behind the enormous cab. I pulled Deuan up behind me. After a moment, the truck rumbled away, with the driver unaware we were behind the cab. There were even hard hats snapped to the side, along with a shovel. We put on the hats, so it looked like we belonged wherever we were going.

Deuan was as ready for anything as I was. I guess I should have expected this, after all she had done with placid determination. I was glad I had met her.

And yes, you guessed it, we rumbled all the way back to Colm's burned-out office and then were waved on to the military base. One of the army men manning the gate gave me a friendly little salute as we went by.

21

The truck worked its way past barracks, parade grounds, and a motor pool or perhaps a junk yard—it was hard to tell which.

We passed an airfield that ran between two steep hillsides—apparently the only place with enough land that could be flattened. Abandoned hangars sat, falling apart, with clumps of reed-like grasses pushing out from the many lines of cracks in the airstrip.

It was a relic from another era, built by another, greater power, now long gone.

Then the road became smaller, heavily forested on both sides, and wound its way up a gradual incline.

There, at the top, was a wide-open area—all red earth, bulldozed to make an area to stage an excavation.

Attention was focused on a point on a steep embankment about 100 meters away, where excavators were clawing away at a point in the hill. Above them, a small mountain rose, with huge trees reaching upwards, paying no attention to the men below.

Deuan and I jumped off the truck as it slowed. She alighted like she was casually stepping down an elegant staircase.

We walked over to a shipping container with a door and windows—clearly the mobile office for the site. Several men were standing in its shadow with their backs to us. I could tell most were the swarthy and short locals, but one was taller, spindly. Then I saw his white arm in the harsh morning sun, and I knew what I was going to find.

The man turned his head slightly as he detected us approaching.

It was Colm.

Alive in the bright sun. Scheming with my money.

"I finally tracked you down," I said, suppressing my shock.

Colm was also stunned to see me. He paused a moment, considering how to handle me. Then he composed himself into a big smile. He was going to be happy to see me.

"Well, only you could have done it," he said. "And on what a day."

Then he noticed Deuan beside me. Colm's eyes widened and he looked genuinely fearful. He motioned the local workers that were with him to leave us.

"Deuan. You, all the staff, will get paid," he said. "That's a promise."

He said it in the way the CEO of a bankrupt company speaks when trying to placate investors. Deuan showed no reaction, but just stared at him.

"Look," he said to both of us. Then there was another pause to decide what to say.

"When my father died," he said. "I found out the details of this. In his papers, this place came to light. I needed the money for the company so I could have access here. So I could find it!"

He stopped to consider what he was saying, looking at both of us one by one. He recomposed his thoughts.

"This was too big and too crazy to tell anyone about, and I had no choice," he said. "That... that sounds crazy, I know. But this was the one time... the one time I could go out and do this. I wanted to take a chance on this. Be lucky for once."

I knew what he meant but did not want to agree with him.

"You have a lot of nerve telling me that," I said. "But I'm going to get my money back. One way or another."

"The money is all tied up in this," he said. "Just wait and you will get your money back and more besides and we will start our school back in Bangkok."

He watched for my reaction.

"Who died in that fire?" I said.

I could see that only now did he realize that I had been surprised to find him here.

"I don't know," he said, smirking. "Only a few are aware of what we are doing here. The fire was too bad. That someone had to die. Maybe an accident. Maybe someone used that to pressure me... and they did use it to pressure you. You smart enough to think of that?"

"I know that people are watching," I said. "That much I do know. And secrets have a bad habit of leaking out."

"You're right," he said. "And once the government catches wind of what we are doing, it's all over."

"You daring me to make trouble?" I said. "You are going to have to do better than that. If we found you, others will too, but I don't care about that. Like you, I'm in it for the money, at the least the money you stole."

I tried to say it in a tough way, but it was a humiliation to be begging for one's own money.

"I don't know what to tell you," he said. "You can see for yourself what is going on here and what I am telling you is true. For now, I have connections just like you apparently do. Those *consultants* are all over this now."

"Consultants?" I said.

Then Colm said conspiratorially to us, "Best you don't know. You will get your money. I promise.

"Everyone," he said, exaggerating the word as he looked at Deuan.

Deuan was oddly contemplative.

"There are a lot of people looking for you," she said. "Your old employees."

"I am going to level with you. There was only enough money to get the company set up and get the mining rights back. I had to move fast. Everyone will get paid. Look, you could cause trouble. Just don't say anything. It won't help get your money back. As far as the soldiers at the base know, as far as anyone knows, we are reviving this mining operation. Bear with me, okay?"

"This is a big gamble. With my money," I said.

"And mine and Matthew's too," he said.

I was momentarily surprised that I had forgotten about our other partner, reticent little Matthew still back in Bangkok.

"Bert, you, more than anyone, should understand this," Colm said. "When I had this chance, this one chance to find the thing, I took it. Yes, I broke the rules, but I figured it out. Seems like you did too. I knew you were smart. That's why I called you after I left. Only you."

He was making too much sense.

Colm leaned towards me. "Use that ticket they gave you. Get out of the country while you can. We'll have our school another day."

After a moment, what he had said dawned on me.

"How do you know I was given a plane ticket?" I asked.

Colm was momentarily blank faced as he searched for the right facial expression to show me.

I turned to the shipping container office next to us. The windows were tinted black as they would be in this climate. I walked over and ascended the three steps to the door. I opened the door. Standing there, in all her spook glory, was Lori.

"So, you are the 'consultant.' Every time, it's a big reveal with you," I said.

She nodded her head for a few seconds, at a loss for words. Finally, she smiled, as though impressed that I had found her.

"You have your ticket," she said. "And you've had your second chance and more than that. I'm leveling with you now. Be on that flight."

"The U.S., my own government, is in cahoots with this guy now?" I said, gesturing to Colm.

She stepped down from the shipping container office to face me.

"No. It is not. Nothing is going on here, except for what you see, which again, is nothing." She said it with authority, like a school teacher setting a child on the right path, but also with a little smile, like I should understand and play along.

"So, everyone's in on this, but me?" I said, looking around. "You got me to find him to get in on whatever this is?"

"Come on. You served your purpose," Lori said. "You did a good thing. Really. But you are not running things. I know you've been involved in some wild stuff. You're capable. But you are not the hero of this story."

Then, maybe not wanting to antagonize me, she added, "You are still free to leave the country, no questions asked. Just go and don't make trouble."

Lori then looked to Deuan and said, "You should not be here, not even be seen here."

"No," Deuan replied, somewhat sadly, "It's you people who should not be here, not now, not then."

"Aren't you taking a chance?" I said to Lori. "I could still raise the alarm."

Somewhat wearily, Lori said, "Don't try it. I told you, I could make trouble too."

"No need for that," Colm said. "He's going to leave. He won't tell anyone."

"Only Bert Mars could have figured all this out," he added, as if to flatter me.

"This is the dream," Colm continued earnestly. "You know that."

I did know exactly what he meant: both of us coming out here, to these places far from our own civilizations, places we could never understand and that did not care to understand us. Places that would probably consume us or maybe, just maybe, give us a lucky break. That's what this all was, a chance to be lucky.

Some local men came over and surrounded Deuan and me in a friendly manner—as friendly as it could be. We were to be escorted out.

"So, this is the way it is," I said.

Lori stood silently in victory.

"It'll be fine," Colm said. He appeared hopefully sincere. "Be on that flight. You'll get your money."

He grinned and reached out his hand to shake mine, but as I made no movement towards him, he turned it into a half-hearted wave.

I should have hit him—it would have been more fitting and dramatic, but I gave him a slight nod instead.

I was in everyone else's power. I should get out of the country now, I knew. At least I knew the truth of what was happening, or at least most of it. It was a race to find the crown before the story got out. Maybe I was the only one who knew all the sides of it.

We were led away to a small pickup truck. One of the construction workers drove us off the base.

"Are you going to report him?" I asked Deuan.

"No," she said, sadly. "It won't change anything."

"Lori, that lady. Does she know you?"

"No," Deuan said. "No one knows me."

I put my hand on hers. I felt sorry she was sad, maybe more than I was sorry for the loss of my money. It was that feeling men have for women sometimes.

It occurred to me that I was not sure what Deuan knew of everything—like the search for the crown. Even Colm, Lori, and the military base—there was some web of interests running in between the raindrops I could only guess at.

I wanted to summon everyone to sit around a table and ask what was really going on, but it was best that I did not know until I had escaped.

If I alerted the authorities, it would probably get me detained or arrested—and the crown, if it were then to be found, would be lost.

Who knows? Maybe Colm would find it and be able to pay me back. No reason to scuttle that. He might be the person to do it. He'd done all this so far. It was a chance at least.

Still, it stung to be sent away. Once, I was sure I was ahead of them all, but I had ended up way behind. I was the only one who was what he seemed, after all.

22

Deuan and I were dropped off back in town where we had jumped on the truck. No one took any notice of us. Maybe I wasn't as important as I thought. In some circumstances, that's for the best.

We went back into the restaurant, and headed to a table, one in an alcove. I wanted to retreat for a moment and regroup my thoughts.

A beer, in a coffee cup, was soon before me. I was going to cut back, but I wasn't going to cut back today.

Deuan was there beside me. I had walked right past her to the table to get a beer and only thought of her again once

I had taken a drink. She tilted her head at me as though expecting me to speak. So, I did.

"They gave me a ticket" —I gestured with it to prove my point— "to leave the country. I tried but I couldn't do anything. I hate to let anyone down—especially you."

"You figured out what was going on," she said.

"And there was nothing to be done," I replied.

"Now you understand my country," she said.

"We both know this," I said with a smile. "It's hard to get ahead."

I took another drink of the beer. It was refreshing but did not taste good. It was a false balm to soothe me and make it okay to slink away, yet I took another drink.

"Don't worry about winning anymore," she said. "Sometimes you have to endure. Patiently."

That is the last thing a young man wants to hear. Yet I knew that was true.

"After all that happened," I said, "I don't think I can come back here again."

"I know," she said. "And that lady was right. I should not be seen around here. And not with you."

We were then silent for a moment, resigned that we were parting.

"You sent me to the temple," I said. "The abbot? He knew about Colm's family. He knew about Colm. All about... this. I think there's more to this, and to you."

"You're likely right," she replied. "I just wanted what I was owed. Like you did."

Women were good at lying.

I could have asked, "Are you with the revolutionaries?" but I knew that once something is said, it cannot be retracted.

"I shouldn't know anything else," I said. "If I was detained again before I left the country, they might be able to get it out of me. It wouldn't be safe for anyone."

All I could do was look into her eyes again, those cool black eyes.

"I didn't expect to meet one like you," she said. "It makes me want to tell you everything."

"Don't," I said.

It was a quiet moment in the alcove where we were sitting. She nodded.

We leaned together, almost imperceptibly.

She looked out furtively to make sure no one was about. And then, we were both leaning forward more, and then we kissed. Not a kiss of passion that leads to nothing, but a genteel kiss that could have led to everything.

"Goodbye, Bert Mars," she said.

"Goodbye, Deuan," I said.

Then, I was walking away down the street. I left her there. I'll think about this when I'm old.

I wasn't sure I had ever told her my last name. Maybe she had seen it on my airline ticket when we flew here.

Things don't work out—there is no karma. We have to look hard for it. Rationalize that it exists. Otherwise living is unbearable.

23

I arrived at the traffic circle with the missing monument. I felt woozy in the hot air. I was considering how I would spin this tale into something other than a failure.

The airport bus stop was there. A bus came by every hour. This was explained in English on a sign there, badly faded from the sun.

Sitting down at one of the open-air shops near the bus stop, a lady there offered me a drink in a metal cup. It was still a holiday, after all. I did not resist. It did not matter now. I'll stop when I get back to Bangkok, I told myself. I would give it up, finally. What I had made of myself and what it would take to stop, flooded my mind. It was sickening. It made me furious that I had let this happen.

I tapped my fingers on the table, on the vinyl tablecloth that caught the beads of condensation from the side of the cup of beer.

I was now anxious to leave. Had to get away. Waiting on this Sunday, a long Sunday. Maybe winning wasn't everything. But I knew people only said this when it was clear they could not win.

I looked up from my metal cup as something large blanked out the bright light of the day.

It was the Keeper—or at least his silhouette—looming before me.

"May I... may I talk with you?" he asked, with his scowling smile.

Not waiting for my reply, he sat down before me, his girthy stomach blocking my exit. I squirmed uncomfortably thinking I might have to flee. He noted my momentary unease.

"No concerns" he said. "That was a misunderstanding before. All forgotten. We understand each other." He waved his hand, sweeping away the past.

"I am on my way to the capital," he continued. "There are always new things to be collected. Maurice will carry on here. Watching."

He said this as though this news should comfort me.

Then he leaned forward, his bulk obscuring my view of the street.

"Did you... did you find it? Really?"

"No," I said.

He studied me for a long moment, so long it revealed his skepticism about everything I said to him.

"Like I said before, I suspect I know you," he said, ignoring my answer. "Your ambition, your drive. Maurice told me about you. Single-mindedness to your goal above all else."

This made me a bit uncomfortable. I had thought of myself like this but did not want my own selfishness to show so easily to others.

"So, if there is someone who might find it, it would certainly be you," he continued. "I have a knack for perceiving amazing things in the everyday. I am always looking, after all."

"No, I found nothing," I said, waving my ticket. "Somebody thinks they know. That's for sure. Just not me. They are packing me off out of the country."

"My boy, the world tells you to be afraid," he said. "That nothing is the same anymore."

I think I nodded involuntarily. I knew what he meant.

"People have always said that," he continued. "And maybe this time it is true; I don't know."

He gave a contemptuous chuckle.

"But I am going to proceed to get what I want," he said. "Maybe all the people won't, maybe you won't, but I will."

He said it gravely, then broke into a friendly and diabolical smile.

"I must leave now," he said. "Things to do."

He stood up and handed me his card. He wheeled around, and, in a few lumbering steps, stepped into a waiting car. The car slowly pulled away and headed down the street in a way somehow as ponderous as the Keeper himself.

I looked at his card. There was no hint of a business on the card, just his long, imponderable name in the local language and his Western name in parenthesis for someone like me—"Bob."

It made me smile. He did not seem like a Bob at all.

I put the card in my pocket, feeling the papers from Colm's office there. I took the papers out of my pocket and unfolded them onto the table. Strange paperwork from another day.

A notation on a photo stood out: "It will be given to the right person."

People had thought I was Colm. Was I Colm or the next best thing? And if Colm found the crown, what would happen? Would finding it mean anything?

What would revolution and multi-party democracy here achieve? More fertile soil for planting? Property taxes for all?

What a thing for an American to think. It was a hard life either way. Maybe I needed to think that to rationalize it all.

The more I thought, the more I knew that Colm had bested me. I was sitting here, cast out of the realm of action and adventure, on my way to the airport.

I flipped through the paperwork. I was again drawn to the photo of the entrance to an old estate and the handwritten translation: "Oungkran Province, see the gold moon—it will be given to the right person."

The photo did not look like the mine area I had just been to. The photo showed a leafy avenue with a mansion partially hidden in the distance.

"...see the gold moon." I read it out loud.

Odd. The gem in the crown was pale blue, not gold. It was the "Moon Gemstone"—with light like the moon. Forever out of reach.

I called over the shop owner, an older lady.

"Could you take a look at this?" I said, pointing out the inscription on the photo.

"Ah, old photo," she said in a way that sounded like she was feigning enthusiasm when dealing with a tourist. "Going there?"

"I've already been, I think," I said.

"My cousins grew up in that village," she said.

"What village?"

The lady said, "'See the gold moon.' It's the name of..."

She was searching for the word.

"Village area. A place name. Yes? That vowel there," she said, pointing to the writhing foreign letters, "is shorthand for something like 'see.'"

"What do you mean?"

"It might be omitted in English. The phrase, in my language, means, it implies, the area is so poor or dry that you can only look up to the moon, yearning. It is a kind of a joking. A joke! The government changed the name to 'Village of Joy,' but no one calls it that."

I looked at the bubble script again, gently swirling before my eyes.

"So 'gold moon' means a place?"

"Yes. The village. 'See the Gold Moon.'"

I knew then. "Oungkran Province, see the Gold Moon" was referring to a location. It was a place.

The gem in the crown was pale blue, after all, not gold. With light like the moon. So "gold moon" or "see the gold moon" did not refer to the crown or the gem itself, but to a village. Maybe only people familiar with this area would even realize it. The crazy pitfalls of language.

So, Colm had probably misinterpreted this. Or who knew why he believed it was in the mine. But now, I was quite sure I had discovered something—something that no one else realized.

I was ahead again.

The note scribbled on these papers so long ago could mean that the "thing"—I was censoring the word even in my thoughts now—was at this poor, dry village of government joy. I shuffled the papers in my hand to one of the receipts with Colm's father's name on it. I compared the letters under his English name—which I guessed was the address—to the letters written on the photo. Yes, the words matched—"See the Gold Moon"—the squiggly language matched. "See the Gold Moon" was a place, not a reference to the crown itself.

Colm's father's old residence had been there. It could be worth checking out, especially with everyone else focused on the old mine site.

"I learned English from my daughters," the shop owner was saying. "Both of my daughters studied in the U.S.A."

She gestured to photos on the wall showing fetching young women receiving their university degrees. One always sees such photos prominently displayed in these countries. It was oddly endearing, a supreme accomplishment that meant something. I could feel her pride as she stood there beaming.

"Oungkran Province, See the Gold Moon—it will be given to the right person."

I looked at the gently rising bubbles in the amber beer. Now I knew something they did not. I smiled devilishly, not concerned if anyone saw me.

24

I gave up waiting for the airport bus and went to where taxis were parked on the other side of the traffic circle.

Johnny was there, the driver with a daughter with a house in Orange County, the driver who had taken us from Colm's burning office. He was leaning against his taxi and smoking his cheap cigarette, as if waiting for me. He was well-dressed, like one who takes even a job of drudgery like this seriously.

He had a moment of confusion when I told him I wanted to go to the "See the Gold Moon" village.

"Why do you want to go there?"

I thought fast.

"I'm writing a book on the history of the area," I said.

I caught myself before mentioning any specific person, like Colm's father, as he was a pre-revolutionary figure. I just needed to say as little as possible.

I showed him one of the receipts from Colm's father with the address, but folded so that only the address written in the local language showed.

"This is where I want to go," I said.

Johnny did not move or reach for the receipt, but I thought I detected some subtle flash in his eyes—some recognition. It was just for a moment, and then it was gone. He remained so calm that it made me think that, if he were more than a driver, he was indeed an expert at lying.

"Sure," he said, as he threw his cigarette down and got into the car.

We drove off and he tried to engage me in conversation.

"You really a writer?" he said, gently mocking me.

"I'm trying," I said.

He said nothing more, although I knew it was unlikely that anyone would want to write about this remote place.

We drove through the rolling terrain, along ravines, and over roads baking in the late-afternoon sun.

This was my last chance to figure all this out, and I was going to take it, with everyone else here smugly thinking I had failed and was slinking away.

"This would make a good story," I said, really to no one in particular.

"It would," Johnny said.

He lit a cigarette. It smelled terrible, even for a cigarette.

At several places, we dipped down and drove across a gravel crossing through a stream.

"In Orange County, they build a bridge over every tiny stream. Rich country," he said, shaking his head.

It was clear that here it was not thought cost-effective to build bridges over every watercourse.

We came out of the ravine and there was a sign showing we were entering a new area.

"Here it is, 'Village of Joy,'" Johnny said, almost a bit wryly, as he stopped the car.

It was a single street with a dozen shophouses along it. A single shop was open—a neighborhood grocery store. A young boy sat in front of it on a crate, staring out onto the hot street.

"This is the place," he said, like I might not have believed him the first time he'd said it.

"Okay, but I want to go to that address I showed you," I said. "It must be somewhere near here. It's an old estate, I think."

This time, he said nothing, but it almost seemed as if he should have asked again why I wanted to go there.

We drove off, past the shophouses and past a collection of small wooden houses on the outskirts of the village, all tilting a bit like they were trying to get out of the sun.

I began to realize that I did not know what I was going to do when I got to the place I was going. Do I just knock on the door of the old family house?

We plunged down into one final ravine and directly into what was left of a once rushing stream.

There was still enough muddy water left to cause the driver to have to pick his way across. Deep ruts carved when the water had flowed at full force made the taxi's tires spin in the slick, silty mud.

Johnny navigated our way confidently, as if this kind of driving was nothing out of the ordinary.

"Cannot pass at all in the rainy season," he said apologetically.

Looming high above us was a half-finished bridge across the stream, with a Chinese-language sign beside it.

In those days, it seemed peculiar that sprawling, chaotic China would want to spend money in small nations like this, but few then understood the emerging outreach China was engaged in, financing and constructing projects for its neighbors like this to extend its influence, like the U.S. had once done.

This place we were going was in the middle of nowhere—a dry nowhere. In a few months, the rains would transform the brown foliage into a fecund green tangle, but for now, piles of dead leaves were everywhere.

Each new road was more overgrown, until finally, we were going down a track along a dense jungle on one side, and, on the other, a field, apparently exhausted, with tall weeds waving in the slight breeze.

There was a slight crease in the road where an overgrown lane branched off into the forest. Johnny stopped. He looked back at me questioningly.

"This is the place," he said.

Two brick pillars, enwrapped in vines, stood on each side of the lane that led into the forest. I got out of the taxi and could just make out a gate overgrown with vines between the two brick pillars.

I walked up to the gate and took out the photo of Colm's father's estate. This was the same place pictured in the photo. The same gate. The only difference was that a more modern-looking chain-link fence was now erected behind the gate.

The original gate had slumped off its hinges, and I was able to push my way past it and break through tendrils that overlay everything. As I tore at the vines and spiders' webs, I realized no one had been through here in a long time.

Turning back, I looked at the driver. He was standing by his taxi in the silence of the evening, watching me expectantly.

I pushed into the tangled lane. With each step, my eyes adjusted to the dimness, and I soon approached the front lawn of an overgrown estate. On one side of the lane was a dark pool with a metal bench at its edge. On the other side was a tangle of fallen trees and vines hanging like ragged curtains. Overhead was the canopy of the forest, covering the little lawn men had once tended.

Beyond was the house, the family mansion. It was peeking out from behind a line of towering broad-leafed plants—something maybe planted long ago and now freed from the continuous taming hands of man to grow into tree-like giants.

The old mansion was only standing because it was cement. Its wooden windows and doors had decayed or maybe had been taken away and repurposed. Rotting piles of plants and broken pottery were scattered everywhere.

I walked up the steps to where the front door once was, and entered. Inside were entwining vines and trees growing up through the floor. The air was deadly still, with shafts of light dropping from above. There was a heavy smell of both living and dead foliage.

A stairway to an upper level had partially collapsed, slumping as though tired. This was a place that would never again be used by man. The jungle was overtaking it, as it would surely do to all our works.

A chair with two legs broken off kneeled beside a collapsed fireplace—hardly a thing one might ever want here in the tropics. Long ago, someone had recreated their

European life here. But it had been no use—nature and history had won.

I was suddenly dejected, as the reality of the world returned. I had made it here, following uncertain clues to a dead land. There was surely nothing to be found.

25

I stepped back outside. It was beginning to get dark, and the mosquitoes were coming out.

A huge black bird leapt off the top branches of a tree and wafted away slowly, like a huge slow-motion bat, a thing of this festering jungle. It looked unreal, huge, and magical.

I wanted to believe I was in control of my destiny, not depending on the government or deities or anyone's rules. I guess I thought I was exceptional. No, I was trying to be exceptional—even that had to be my decision. And my decisions had brought me here among the dead, dry leaves and ruins of another era. A dead end so far away.

I walked away from the ruins of the house and back onto the front lawn.

I looked up at the heavily forested hills peeking over the trees.

With every step, I seemed to be further away from my own land. And not towards the hope of new business in Asia. I was here in this remote dead place. I had turned over my money to start a school. Now it was gone, all gone. It was hard to get ahead. Especially when you were dumb. It was tiring to be thinking, always thinking, even when I was so alone and so far away.

Then, I felt a presence. It grew from that mysterious power each person has that tells them they are being watched.

I froze, expectant. Maybe the feeling was from some nearby and disturbing silence, some deadening of the soundscape, disturbed by another human presence.

I turned my head cautiously, not too fast and not too slowly, fearing I might startle whatever it was, or maybe startle myself.

Among the leafy bushes beside me were two wide eyes. They were human eyes. After a moment, I was able to make out a crouching figure in the fronds and vines.

A human rose up, as if uncoiling, and moved towards me on legs like an insect, thin and steady and alien in its gait.

I felt as though I was seeing this from far away and from another time, just as you are seeing me now, with my ghost watching over your shoulder.

The figure coming towards me was some kind of man—a feral figure dressed in clothes stained dark red with clay. His eyes were bright, clear and probing.

He approached me, and, instead of speaking, put his hand firmly on my arm. He squinted his eyes at me and struggled to speak like he had not spoken for a long time.

"It's you," he said. "You found your way here."

He smiled as his eyes glistened with tears. His hoarse voice was clearing as he spoke.

"They were here, but I didn't give it to them."

I looked at him in incomprehension and amazement, and he continued.

"Word went out... from the abbot," he said.

I was still looking quizzically at him.

"Yes, they said the time had come. You had arrived. But even the abbot did not know where it really was..."

The man peered out of his dishevelment at me. There was recognition. Then he spoke more clearly.

"I am caretaker here, the last guardian," he said, whispering the final word.

"Thank you," I said. I was playing along, not quite sure what was happening.

"They were all here already, over the many years," he said clearly in English, "but I was waiting for you. I knew him, your father, and I kept it safe.

"We heard your dear father passed and you were here. He loved playing here when he was a boy. I knew it was time, the time you were drawn here, on this festival, on the full moon. Finally."

Tears glistened in his eyes. His face opened to me, as he knew who I was, and his reserve of feeling welled up. The lines in his face became expressive with the fulfillment of his mission.

"It's here?" I said. "Not at the mine at the military base?"

"Only for a time it was there, and long ago, it was entrusted to me for safekeeping," he said. "Even today, few in our network know where it really is. And over the years, all those who knew, died—one way or another—and now there is me. And you—as you have found your way home."

I was alert, understanding all he was implying. Even the jungle around us seemed expectant now.

The man led me down a hidden path to a small hut—his own, apparently. He grabbed a rusty shovel and handed me a flashlight. He was no longer hunched over. His moment of action after long years of waiting had arrived.

He got on a motorcycle and motioned me onto the back impatiently. One of my rules for safe travel in their foreign countries was never to ride on a motorcycle, but I was always breaking this rule.

He gestured that I was to hold the flashlight ahead of us, as the bike had no light.

We sailed down a little path, palm fronds smacking against me as we rode along in the gathering dark.

We arrived at a glade with what looked like a line of outhouses, all overgrown and disused. Several were partially collapsed, and all were covered with vines.

The caretaker led me to the far end of the glade, under a huge net of vines. He scanned the area, looking towards the latrines, seemingly counting in his mind. Then verifying the spot, he fell to his knees and prayed.

He stood up and looked towards the old latrines and then back to me. Almost apologetically, he said, "It is a good hiding place." And he began to dig.

He quickly pulled up a couple of rotten wooden planks. Under these was a hollowed-out area with a bundle resting inside.

The man got out of the hole, gesturing to me.

"I dare not touch it. And I will not look upon it," he said. He backed away, continuing to gesture at me and towards the hole.

I got into the hole and pulled out the bundle. The man crouched some way away, returning to his insect-like posture, watching intently. When he noticed me looking at him, he slowly and servilely retreated into the thick jungle.

The bundle was composed of layers of canvas and burlap, some of which were brittle and fell away as I unwrapped them.

I found the seam of a burlap bag which was sewn up, and ripped it open. Inside was a rough-hewn clay pot, as red as the dirt of this clay land. It was about the size of an oblong football.

There was an ornamental seal on one side. It looked like a squiggle, one of their language's letters. It almost made me a bit sad, for some reason. Something that once meant power, receding in time.

I cradled this thing now, the thing everyone wanted, the thing that had the power of change. It was light as a feather, but I could feel some shifting of objects inside.

And then the wind blew. It was that false hope of the tropics, moments after the sun dipped away at sunset with the sky still radiant, both with color and with heat, and there was that breeze, a titter of excitement. But it was never anything but a tepid wind, bringing no cool, a reminder of what might be, but will not be on this day.

I slowly pried open the lid of the pot. It was sealed with some material that had long ago hardened.

There were packets inside, fabric quilted packages. I opened one. I then opened another.

"Quickly," the old feral man called from somewhere nearby.

Some of the packets contained rice. But not all of them.

"Quickly," he said again, now in a commanding tone.

Not even the abbot had known exactly where it was. He too had thought it was in the mine. But their network had gotten out the word. I had arrived. I was here. The right person was here.

I was in moonlight now. The clouds had blown away, and the moon was there, everyday and incredible.

I put the lid back on and put the pot back in the burlap bag. I held it close as I returned to the motorcycle. The man emerged from hiding, almost in a panic now. He drove us back down the path to his hut.

He dropped the motorcycle to the ground as we got off, and, grabbing me by the arm, showed me to an overgrown path. He was growing frantic, and this rubbed off on me. I wanted to get to someplace safe.

I had to duck under the fronds and leaves that were stretching out across the path. I imagined they were trying to prevent my escape. Any minute, Lori or Maurice or the invisible authorities watching me might pop out. Or Colm might appear to show that I was an imposter.

The caretaker was waving me ahead, and, in a moment, I realized why. In the otherwise quiet of the evening, I could clearly hear a voice, speaking on an amplified speaker, perhaps a police radio, and then the crackling of tires of vehicles on gravel. They were coming.

Suddenly, we stumbled out of the forest and were back at my taxi, still waiting at the gate.

I put my hand on the man's shoulder to say goodbye. He seemed the type that was linked to the place, like one who must not leave the border of his forest.

He took my hand and shook it awkwardly and smiled. He smiled like someone who thought times could change.

"Well done, you have been faithful," I said, attempting to say something that would be meaningful to him.

He could not find words to reply to me. This fellow surely believed that there would now be an uprising of the farmers and their families on barren lands. It made me hopeful for myself too. I felt his history and his expectations, at least on this day.

He backed away from me, merging once again into the paths of the jungle that he knew so well.

Fool that I was, I had taken a chance. I had followed the clues again, and it had made me lucky. I was the right person after all. I wondered if this was my magical fate. Once one starts believing, magical things begin to appear everywhere.

26

I got back in the taxi, looking around for the vehicles I was hearing.

"What's going on?" I asked.

"They are coming," Johnny said nervously, with a forced smile.

"Who?"

He shrugged and began driving away calmly, continuing on the road along the edge of the forested area.

"Who?" I shouted, getting a bit panicky.

Then, I heard the ah-ooga wail of a police siren nearing. And Johnny was continuing on like he heard nothing, very slowly.

"Let's get going!" I yelled.

He said, "Don't worry."

But it was now clear he was taking me down the road directly to whoever was coming. I could see a plume of dust rising in the moonlight in the near distance. They were almost upon us.

"Not this way!" I shouted, banging on the back of his seat.

"Hold on," Johnny said. This was serious now.

I was going to have to make a decision. I was sure I was about to be captured. I had to do something. The sword does not ask why it is sharp, after all. This is what I was made for. I had to make myself lucky again.

The taxi was moving slowly, almost slowing to a halt, as though anticipating the approach of whatever authorities were onto me. I was not going to be caught like this. I opened the taxi door and jumped out with the burlap bag, stumbling a little.

I stood on the road, jungle to my left, a field of tall weeds to my right. I looked all around. I wondered if it was practical to try to outrun whoever was after me now. It was all dense jungle and heat. There seemed finally no place left to escape to.

Then, a small helicopter screamed over me and plopped roughly into the middle of the road ahead. A scrawny old pilot, in shorts and flip flops, slid out and ran over to me, handing me a paper. I unfolded it.

It read, "He will fly you back. I will meet you in the capital. Maurice."

It was written in a flowery hand, and I could almost hear Maurice saying the words. People were indeed watching.

A phalanx of official cars of some kind appeared ahead, on the other side of the chopper. Something was being screamed over a loudspeaker. It was in a foreign tongue, but I could make out two English words, "Cease!" and "Halt!"

I ran to the chopper. The rotors were still thumping as I jumped in.

I clutched the burlap bag in my lap and waved to Johnny. He was now standing beside his taxi impassively and smiled back dumbly as the chopper tilted away from the ground.

We shot up, taking my breath away and wheeling over the jungle, quickly putting me out of sight of the approaching vehicles.

We looped around the old estate and its guardian, hidden in the fronds somewhere below. I was sure he was seeing this.

I held on for dear life as I recalled the crashed helicopter back in Bangkok. It seemed long ago when I was taking an air-conditioned taxi to a high-class hotel to pick up a briefcase of money.

I had wanted something to happen and now it was happening.

After a few minutes, it was clear we were headed back to the capital, over steep, mountainous terrain. We zoomed along a row of towering power pylons, using the lines as a guide, the lines no doubt coming from the hydroelectric dams in the mountains, sending electricity back to the capital, where we were heading, and then on to Thailand, where power was sold to needy modern industry.

The sky was black and terrifying, but we flew along in the moonlight, with the power lines at our right always guiding us, piloted by an old man in flip flops.

I remembered stories of men who fell out of choppers in these far countries when they had outlived their usefulness. But it was only me and a scrawny-looking pilot.

The pilot was impassive, perhaps used to speed in the night. He looked a bit bored.

My hair stood on end as we flowed through the blackness. My elation made me feel like I was either alive or perhaps dead, in the few final moments after we had met with a towering hillside. But no, I thundered on, like a God above a sickly world.

Below, in places here and there, were dots of light, people awake, reading, studying, watching TV, farmers with their babies on the barren hillsides. I had visions of these people like one used to have when train travel was the fashion—imagining the lives of those I was quickly passing, dots of light, on one of the nights of my life.

It made me think of Deuan and the mysteries between us.

I had to decide my next move. I wished it was a consequential decision of good and evil, where, at a high place, having been offered the world, I could say no, I reject temptation. But no. It was nothing like that. Any consideration I made would be uncertain, with risks both good and evil. It was a decision that I had to make. And yes, I made it.

The moon was noble on this arresting night, contrasting with the crass things we men were doing.

We landed at a tiny helipad in a field in the capital. The pilot suddenly became agitated. I got the sense that someone was supposed to be there to meet me, but no one was around. I realized this was my chance to get away.

The pilot spoke to me frantically, finally grabbing my arm as I tried to get out.

"Thanks," I said, pretending that I misunderstood his panic.

I jumped out, thinking he might take off again to prevent me from exiting. I ran off as he shouted at me.

I knew that the border was closed until morning and there were no flights overnight, so I went right to the street bar where I had first found Andrew. And he was there, of course.

He grinned as if he were expecting me.

"Fancy a beer?" he said.

Yeah. Yeah, I did.

27

It was very early that Monday morning, still dark, when I checked back into the old palace hotel—a place of historical character that Westerners would appreciate while locals would criticize for not being brightly lit and made from cement—you see, anything old and wooden must be loaded with ghosts of the past.

They put me back into the same room I had had when I first checked in the previous Friday. It was the room where Maurice had held me at gunpoint before I had even heard of the crown. That seemed like many years ago.

Being back in the same room was comforting. It made me think, "It will be fine." I lay down on the bed pondering my weekend and closed my eyes.

I dreamed I was a giant walking down a road, but my train of thought was interrupted by a dog barking, distracting me.

The dog was barking and I wished he would be quiet. I recalled a study that showed that smaller breeds barked pointlessly hour after hour with no purpose. Stupid dogs.

Then I was no longer a giant. I couldn't get on my flight. I had lost my ticket. I was mad at everyone. This was why I shouldn't travel.

I woke up and was more tired than when I had gone to sleep. I had that sickening feeling of being up too early in the morning, everything expectant, still under the altered state of dreams, knowing that in the morning, things could go well or ill, randomly.

I got out of bed and opened the blackout blinds. The morning sun was already signaling it was going to be a hot day. I tried to shake off the remnants of the dream.

Outside was a small lawn, enclosed by white walls. The white of the walls was shockingly white in the morning sun. There was no indistinct mood here; the sun was bright all day, clarifying every bright line, sharp and vivid and hot. There was no noir in these countries.

An old man was toiling away on the green lawn in the first rays of the sun, dreaming dreams of revolution maybe, while others wanted the past buried or just to profit from it. And for some, it was only a means to an end, another thing to chase, but probably never reach.

There was a knock on the door. It was just after 6 am and cocks were crowing outside. I was growing confident in the morning and opened the door.

A nervous Maurice entered, as if this was his room. He nodded at me pleasantly in greeting.

"Morning. Pardon the interruption," he said.

Then Lori followed, almost pushing him out of the way. She was a bit too commanding and confident, like she was the one in charge.

I looked at her and said, "I'm somehow not surprised to find you right in the middle of things again."

"And I'm almost impressed with you now," she said back to me. I got the feeling she knew I had beaten her.

Then Colm himself appeared, smiling uncertainly as though he were testing my reaction to him. I didn't even think of slugging him. I smiled back.

"So, it's here?" he said, really hopefully, but also with an undercurrent of annoyance. He was pretending to be pleasant, although I had shown him up. It was great. Or maybe this was how I wanted to see it. It was too early in the morning.

I just shrugged back at him.

"Here. Here it is," Maurice said with a gasp of excitement. He had found the pot in the burlap bag, sitting on the bedstand.

"You came right here from the chopper?" Lori asked, pointing at me. She was interrogating me like a cop would.

"Yes, he came right here," Maurice said. "He was never out of our sight."

Lori weighed that.

Then Maurice sniffed at me, "Going back to the same hotel. Audacious."

"Now that everyone thinks they know everything," I said, "I'll ask: Who was chasing me at the estate last night?"

"The government. The party," Lori said. "Not the provincial police. You just missed being arrested."

"No one could have helped you then," Colm said. He grinned like he was happy to be letting me know I had been dumbly lucky.

"Let's make this quick," Lori said, gesturing to the pot in annoyance.

"Yes, let's see it," Colm demanded.

No one cared they had barged into my room. No one was asking my permission, but I decided to let them think I was the lucky dupe that they thought I was.

All this was going to happen.

Maurice was holding the burlap bag as though surprised he had finally found it.

Lori asked, "Is it... is it sealed?"

"Yes, this is the vessel. It has the seal," Maurice said. He had reached into the bag and drew out the pot. He pointed to the seal I had first seen yesterday in the moonlight. The group let out a collective hum of agreement and leaned forward almost menacingly.

It had all come down to this. We were all graspingly desperate. All of us and our conflicted allegiances.

Maurice was suddenly fearful. "You... you open it," he said to me and sat the pot down in the bed. They gathered around.

When I had checked in last night, I had borrowed some paste glue from the hotel front desk to reseal the pot. It still had an area on one side of the lid where some of the pottery had cracked off when I first opened it, but I kept that side to me. This was working.

Someone banged on the door. An American-accented voice on the other side said, "Move it along. We don't have much time."

Lori replied back, "Almost done."

Everyone peered at the pot I cradled in my hands. I popped open the lid and made sure it made a satisfying crack.

Maurice suddenly put both hands on the pot and firmly pulled it away from me.

"It was still sealed," he said.

He reached in and pulled out a fabric packet. He roughly tore it open. He poured it out and fragments of rice fell on the bedspread.

Maurice pulled out more sewn packets. He pulled them open, scattering rice on the bed. Then another and another.

"It is all rice samples. Desiccated rice," Maurice said with disappointment.

No one was looking at me, but I tried to look disappointed too.

"Am I going to be compensated for this?" I asked. "I found it, right?" I had to make this look good.

Colm looked on grimly.

"Better luck next time," he said. He was happy and maybe relieved now that I had not done what he could not.

"No hard feelings," Colm said. "I'm still going to search at the mine. It's still out there somewhere!"

"You're surely the right person to find it," I said.

"I... I'm sorry," Colm said. "I know this has been hard. I never thought it would be like this. I think you understand somehow. I will make it up to you—to everyone. It'll be fine."

I allowed myself to smile at him.

"I do understand," I said. "I understand it all."

Lori was momentarily annoyed. It was the confusion and ire of someone who thought they knew what was going on. I was reading her mind and she was thinking, "Idiot!" but she was not sure if I or she was the idiot.

But all she said to me was, "Well, lucky for you, you didn't find it."

I wanted to ask what that meant. Would there have been a free-for-all for the crown among all these people with separate loyalties? Or was it something else?

"Time to go, Mars—now," Lori said. "For your own safety. I won't be able to help you again. Your luck has run out."

She looked at me one last time with her alluring gaze, somehow expressing that I had disappointed her for not bringing her the crown.

I tried to look crestfallen as she turned and left the room.

"Yeah, the news of your aerial escape is spreading," Colm said. "When the government boys wake up and decide to get to work, they will be beating down your door."

"I'm on my way," I said, grabbing the few things I had brought with me.

Maurice moved to the door after the others left, and gently pushed the door closed so he could say something to me privately.

"So, my employer..." Maurice said. "He will remain disappointed, I assume? It will not disappear into his hands... or any other?"

I paused, contemplating how forthcoming I should be.

"Where did you go last night?" Maurice asked kindly, as if he expected I would confide in him.

I looked at him calmly and said, "I came directly here. You can see from the check-in time."

I didn't expect he would check it. He was still looking at me as he pondered. He had a tired look in his eyes, almost like those men farming on the hillsides.

"Very well," he said.

I guess he believed me. Maybe I was becoming a better liar.

Still, I couldn't resist asking. "You weren't watching me the whole time since I returned, and yet you told them you were."

"My dear boy," he said. "Revolution is the longest and most improbable thing. It is a mission I have been pursuing a long time.

"The truth is..." and he sighed, "if you had found the crown, it would not matter. It is perhaps the province of hopeful fools... like me. It is not the right time. The people are uneducated, asleep. There is discontent, but the day has not yet arrived when we can regain our land.

"There is personal danger to myself from several quarters." He thought for a moment. "I will forever be a patriot, but also a realist, as all patriots must be when facing injustice and the way things are. It is my eternal frustration."

"And you believed I might be able to find it," I said. "How did you know where I was to send the chopper?"

"You might be surprised of our people. Our divided loyalties. So, it is better that this thing that means so much, but cannot make a difference now, does not fall into the hands of my employer."

"The Keeper," I said.

"Yes, or the government or even hopeful patriots like myself. It would only be lost now, if revealed. Do not speak," he said, holding up his finger.

"I need not know anything, but that our revolution will have to wait for another day. We are not the valorous men we imagine we are. We can only hope that whoever finds it does the right thing for this land and its people."

"You," he said, "can bestride worlds. You can leave this land. You ignorant little boy. Forgive me, I only have this land and my dreams for it."

I understood. We all have dreams that will never come true.

"I hope there are better days ahead," I said. I felt like putting my hand on his shoulder and saying something to cheer him up, but these people did not touch each other like that, and I probably would have babbled something that would lead him to ask more questions.

"We owe a debt to you for the kindness, the respect you afforded to Milady," he said.

"Milady?" I asked.

"There is fate still, even in this world of giant hydroelectric dams." Maurice chuckled grimly. "You were meant to be here, at this time. Well, that is our belief.'

Milady. The way she was treated at the shrine.

"You mean Deuan? Her?" I said. I dropped all pretense of knowing everything that was going on.

"She is in the line. The line that was long ago deposed," he said. "Deposed royalty."

"I don't believe it. Why is she allowed to walk around? Be free? Wouldn't they arrest her?"

"She is now rehabilitated and part of the lowly proletariat. A great victory for the party and a lesson for the people. But she is what she is, despite ideology. And even in our government, there are those sympathetic to the old days."

"How? How did she know about Colm?"

"People know when things are happening. When the aide of the old regime, Colm's father, died, and Colm returned, our network was aware."

"So, she knew?"

"I do not presume to know Milady's mind," he said. This meant something to Maurice. I was touched by his deference to her.

"Well, this is something," I said, at a loss for words.

"I used to say, we will meet again, but that was before I became resigned to my fate," Maurice said. "We will not meet again. I hope you will continue to have... an audacious life."

He smiled warmly and shook my hand firmly. He opened the door and turned around one more time in the doorway—his tiny frame standing proudly and defiantly.

"Goodbye, Bert Mars," he said.

He vanished into his land and his pursuits.

Revolution. No one knows the day and hour, until it suddenly arrives.

This was not that day and not that hour.

I grabbed all my things and left the room. Time to escape.

28

I had to get moving. I left the hotel and walked a bit down the street to hail a taxi to the airport, not wanting to be seen standing in front of the hotel where it was known I had been staying.

An older-model car pulled to the curb. Deuan's placid face looked out at me from the back seat.

I opened the car door and got in. She motioned with authority to the driver to drive.

Deuan was the same lady I knew, but now her face was distant from me.

"We found each other again," she said.

"What are the odds?" I replied.

"Your hotel—the palace—was in my great grandmother's family," she said.

"And your grandfather in the camp?"

"He would have been a prince in the old regime. But instead, he is a reformed farmer—even supportive of the government that had destroyed his family. Until he objected to one of their hydroelectric projects."

"I hope I haven't put you in any danger," I said. "But somehow I suspect not."

"My existence, as an office worker is a symbol of their success of rehabilitation. Same for my late father as he toiled away in a government office issuing driver's licenses."

"But you will be alright?"

"I may have gone too far," she said, looking out the car window. "Perhaps I will be in a camp with my grandfather. This is my karma. But thank you for your kindness."

She was cool and remote.

"I'm leaving quickly—seems I have to," I said.

"Leave..." she repeated, mulling over my words with a hint of bitterness.

"Where is it?" she asked. "You did find it, right? You're going to take it away from us?"

I could tell she wasn't quite sure if I had found the crown or not.

"It wasn't there," I said. "Only moldy rice."

She tilted her head, "I don't know about you. Maybe you are too slippery. Maybe you are too cunning."

"I hope I am," I said.

Then, from out of nowhere, she had a gun on me once again.

"But maybe not cunning enough," I said.

It was a menacing black revolver, too far from me and held too assuredly for me to try to grab it. She was all business again.

"What do you think of the symbols of my country? A toy?" she said. "What do you think of anything?"

Looking down the barrel, I oddly felt little fear. I had been through so much with her. We both knew each other, despite not really knowing anything.

"Where is it? Really," she repeated.

"What can come of this? I said. "Are you sure it is the right time for the crown to appear?"

"Who are you to say?" she said, with a flash of anger.

"I'm just a man who wants to win," I said, leveling with her.

"I believe you, finally," she said. "But you should consider what you are without all the things you think you want."

That hit me for a moment. Maybe it was just the kind of sentiment that would reach a young Westerner like me.

"I'm just a tourist, I guess," I said. "Who are you?"

She looked at me sadly.

"Just the office manager, just a country girl," she said. "At least now, in this time and place."

"Whatever it is, whatever it was, it's too late now," I said. "It's not the right time. I think you know that. The world here... of business, of politics, of revolution, of us. It's a dream for a future day. Some other age."

She nodded subtly, then, after a moment, she lowered the gun.

"My land is asleep. It remains so," she said.

"We will endure then," she added, in a whisper.

I imagined she was thinking of the men and women of the clay, the dams and flooded villages, and her grandfather in a camp. I was.

The car stopped. We had arrived at the airport. At least she still cared enough about me to help me escape.

I regarded her one last time. She was someone else now, or always had been, remote and marvelous. And like so many women I had cared for and loved, someone I perhaps never appreciated until events cast us apart.

"Get out, Bert Mars," she said, gesturing with the gun, but not pointing it at me.

I wanted to say something meaningful, but all I could say was, "I will always remember our trip to Oungkran Province.... and you."

I tried to sound sincere, because I was sincere and I wanted her to know it, but after all the things that had happened, I was afraid I would start sounding like I was always lying. She said nothing in reply.

I looked into her eyes again, one last time, but now she was far away.

"Goodbye, Milady," I said, stepping out of the car.

She made no further sign to me. I closed the car door and she was gone.

So many betrayers. And now I was one. I hoped Deuan would not hold it against me. I could not help her. I could not help anyone but myself, it seemed.

She was another girl I had once kissed. After all that had happened, maybe there could have been a better parting. She was a girl, after all, and I was a boy, but that was all.

Like Maurice said, there was no chance. Not now. Not in this life.

I was dashing their hopes, her hopes. The decision had been made. I was sure it was right, but I was also sure it might be wrong.

29

You can probably guess that I had a plan. No matter how things went, at least I had a plan. I could still make the second leg of my flight today. Lori had me booked on the cheapest flight, which only went over the border to the nearest provincial airport in Thailand. That was fine with me.

I had to pump myself up and think how lucky I was. That was my superpower. My dumb superpower. But I was not out of the country yet.

There were smart people all around—clearly smarter than me. Might some of them begin to think this was all too easy? Why would I carry the unopened pot back to the same hotel so they could all come and see that there was nothing to be found?

I checked in to my flight. All was in order. I was growing confident about my escape. Standing there as the lady checked me in, I looked out over the vacuous blank airport that emphasized to the traveler the richness of the experience they were leaving behind and what they risked by venturing into the skies.

Still, I got the feeling I should be worried. Airports made me worry.

A friendly lady in uniform approached me and asked me to follow her. I was ushered into an interview room.

Several police and military men were waiting for me around a table. And—to my profound shock—one of them was Johnny. Johnny, my driver from Oungkran Province who had taken Deuan and me to the burning office. Johnny, proud of his daughter's house in Orange County.

He was now in military uniform and seated confidently at the table. He seemed pleased to surprise me. A stack of papers was before him. It gave me the impression that the papers contained information about my activities in their jolly squiggly script.

I had taken Johnny to the See the Gold Moon village. I had found him at the traffic circle, and in my friendliness had chosen him to take me there. He must know everything. What a feckless fool I was.

"You are moving up in the world," I said, putting on a brave face. "What should I call you now?"

He had plenty of decorations on his neatly pressed uniform.

"I'm still Johnny," he said, in a genuinely sincere way, as though the implication that he could be someone else was hurtful.

He extended his arm, gesturing for me to sit down. It was friendly enough, but it was also an order.

I tried to act casual, but as I pulled out the chair, it made a loud screeching sound as it moved across the floor. It was the sound of unease.

Johnny removed a cigarette from a pack of Marlboros and took a drag with satisfaction.

"We have no need of that crown," he said. He said it with utter confidence, but still, I could see the other men wince, and one looked over his shoulder. Maybe they had me, but I suspected he was trying to scare or impress me with his openness. This gave me a tiny bit of hope.

"Some of my countrymen may find something compelling about it. But that is not what I am interested in. I am interested that all people have enough."

He was telling me that he was a faithful ideologue.

I considered saying something Deuan would have wanted to say, something about the development of the dams in the hills. People in camps. The hypocrisy of a political system that had been tried so many times in so many countries and that always led to such suffering. But I was also trying to get away. It was time to be humble. To put my sense of Western superiority to the side. I held my tongue.

I could now see my old driver Johnny for what he really was—a poised man in uniform who could deal with a person like me. Most of the people in these countries were men of their time who valued their ways of deference. Talkative and opinionated foreigners from developed nations were considered impolite, unusual creatures, bold and foolish.

These countries needed men like my driver who were not afraid to face someone like me. And I could see he was not afraid of confronting me.

"You only wanted to follow me to see who would turn up in the hunt for the crown," I said.

"Many, many..." he began enthusiastically, then corrected himself. "Just a few," he said, "still assign relevance to this thing."

"And they will be identified and arrested?"

"You Americans are so literal, so crass. Of course, we won't do that. We want to know who they are—everyone involved. They will be monitored—for their own good. Anyone misbehaving will be educated. We care about the people."

He looked me in the eye, challenging me. My alarm bells were going off, but I tried to hide my fear. I could worry about this again one day, once I got away.

During his time in Orange County, Johnny had learned not to be afraid of Westerners, who he learned were really no different than he was. So, coming back, and now in the intelligence community, he could pretend to be a reticent, retiring local man. But inside, he was really an Orange County man, now probably more American than I was. He was the perfect man to deal with someone like me—look at me with his steely gaze and know whether I was lying or not. That is what I imagined, as he leaned over the table towards me and smiled his smile of triumph.

"Even if the crown," he said, and one of the other men looked around nervously again, "was there, the people's government does not care. It means nothing. Our country is too small. Its population too isolated. Everyone is working hard and getting by. That area has been searched. It all has. Don't worry. There is nothing to find."

"I didn't find anything," I said. "It was a crock of moldy rice."

The men laughed unexpectedly, as if we were having a drink together and I had said something funny.

"We know everything already," he said.

I wondered which of the people in the room when we opened the pot was secretly informing on me. Maybe Maurice? The men who accompanied Lori?

My mind was spinning, considering whether I had used everyone or if maybe I was the one who had been used.

"The old caretaker will be taken care of and reeducated," Johnny said, almost like this should scare me.

"This thing—it did not matter to us." He waved his hand dismissively. Now I could detect he was trying to convince me that they did not care, and neither should I.

I considered answering with something like, "It was worth a shot," but I was afraid of extending this questioning and letting on I knew more than they did. They needed to think they were two steps ahead of me. I was a dumb tourist. I just wanted to get on that plane.

Then I was thoroughly searched. I tried to be patient.

I recalled that Johnny had told me he visited his daughter in Orange County every year. That did not seem likely for a taxi driver in this closed-off country. But more likely for a government man. Seems he slipped up a bit in revealing that, but it didn't matter; I hadn't realized it until now. I laughed at myself.

When they saw I had nothing, Johnny became a bit apologetic and friendly again.

"We have to follow every thread to its end. For the people," he said.

"Yeah, I understand," I replied.

He was standing, as was I, and he grabbed my shoulder and turned me a little towards him. He looked directly in my eyes in a steely way.

"If I were a man who could do anything, go anywhere," he said. "You know what I would do?"

I paused to think of a hardboiled thing to say, but before I could, he said, "I would not interfere in issues I can't possibly understand. Wouldn't risk it."

All the men were grinning at me. They thought this a clever thing to say.

"Well, it's a little too late for that now," I said to Johnny.

He returned to his spot at the table. I was certain it was all over for me, due to the paperwork they had before them. Papers to prove things against me.

Still, I tried to look bemused. I was an innocent tourist leaving after a delightful holiday in their unique country.

"You can go. Go," Johnny said, to my surprise.

I paused, but he really wanted me to leave. He was subtly nodding to me. Kind of a motion that said, "Go on." Shooing me away.

Some of the men began talking in their own language, which sounded to me like there was some disagreement about me leaving.

My driver, Johnny, the Orange County man, glanced at me with the very slightest of expressions—a momentary flaring of the eyes. Giving me a chance. This had grown in my mind since the chopper found me at the estate and since Maurice had told me of men sympathetic to the old ways. I realized, maybe guessed, that Johnny must have some of these sympathies despite his rank. Could it be? Because

Johnny was the only person who could have alerted Maurice and the patriots that I was going to the old estate. And he had driven slowly and had not resisted my escape in the chopper.

I wondered if he was thinking of his daughter's house in Orange County and the life she led there—a life in which she rarely had to worry about what she thought or said.

In the end—Johnny, my driver, spy, government man, holder of a Certification in Biology—was perhaps a secret revolutionary. Yet I would never know for sure. I quickly left the room.

As I was doing so, more uniformed men arrived right outside the room. They were talking, eyeing me. It gave me the sense that Johnny, who had just let me go, was being overruled. I began to think I should have never checked in at the airport.

I would be back in a cell with Charhadi, the drug dealer, and, unlike him, I would be very aware that I had foolishly walked into my fate.

It seemed that any minute a higher-up might say they wanted me questioned further. My story could fall apart. I did not want to wait in line in immigration now with all this going on.

More of these men's eyes were now on me. Any moment, I might be called back.

I worked my way into the thickest crowd of people I could find, trying to disappear. I had been pretty cool this whole time, but I was starting to feel the need to flee.

I found a side exit to an outside smoking area. They still had them then. I slipped over the railing that separated the smoking area from the parking lot and found a motorcycle taxi. It sped me away from the airport.

We zoomed through the city, past the street of bars where Andrew whiled away his days, past the old palace hotel where secret patriot Maurice had first confronted me, and past the empty office where Deuan had held a gun on me—with Colm's father's ashes still waiting patiently on the desk.

It was still a sleepy capital, its streets now being baked by the rising sun, while legions of old cars and motorcycles began their ceaseless travels.

I arrived at the border bridge on the river where foot traffic could exit the country and reenter Thailand. I was close to escape.

The bridge had been underwritten by foreign nations under an agreement that the countries involved harmonize their road traffic and allow car and truck travel between their nations.

Alas, as the bridge had neared completion, this small nation had built a parking structure on its side, explaining that no vehicles from Thailand would be allowed on their roads after all, but instead could conveniently be housed in the new parking structure for a fee. This had left the bridge as a white elephant for years, mainly used for border foot traffic and the occasional high-level motorcade.

I began crossing the bridge on foot on my way back to Thailand. A smattering of locals and tourists were crossing in both directions—some vendors carrying bundles of clothes and foodstuffs on their backs and a few ragged tourists in the sun. It was going to be a hot day.

Shuffling across the bridge, matching my gait to the backpackers so as to not appear anxious, I watched over my shoulder the whole way. I told myself it was time to smile inwardly, breathe peacefully and be victorious.

I had heard stories of the immigration checkpoint here being closed at random times, but luckily, it was open today.

The immigration office was a small structure built on the bridge. Inside were desks with stamps and paperwork with grim men and women shuffling through the pages of passports on which to enter their ragged exit stamp.

This was before the U.S. underwrote every tiny country, friend or foe, to install a standard computerized entry system so they could adhere to watch lists of people the U.S. wanted to find. This system also allowed local governments to enforce their own blacklists.

I was not sure if I could have been on a watch list already, to be held and sent back for more questioning. However, my passport was examined cursorily and stamped by an official who was constantly sniffing. In such a job, he probably had a cold all the time.

I was breathing heavily and my hand trembled a bit, but I kept a placid look on my face.

The passport was returned, and I went to the next little building on the Thai side, and was duly stamped into Thailand.

My elation was rising as I walked the rest of the way across the bridge as it descended to the other side of the river and to freedom in Thailand. I was anxious to melt into its legions of foolish tourists. No one would suspect where I had been or what I had done.

There were other directions I could have taken. But what happened, had happened. No need for hugs or affirmation. Just try and try. That's the life of a man. I was still learning this. Never mind, as the Thais liked to say.

I reentered the land of temples and expressways and 7-11s on every corner. A land of teeming concrete sprawling out in every direction. This was my world—capitalistic and corrupt and vibrant in every way possible.

30

That evening, with sundown approaching, I found my way back to the river's edge about 10 kilometers from the border bridge. It was near a popular local beer bar.

I stood on the Thai bank, looking back across to where the young men planted crops on steep red hills. Where an old bureaucrat abbot hoped for change. Where the old caretaker, the guardian of the crown, had done his duty. Where Deuan's dreams and our time together endured.

I wondered what she was thinking now and what fate would befall her. But I was sure she would weather whatever would happen. I recalled her calm and steely glance and knew she would endure, and perhaps prevail.

Worlds would forever separate us as time moved on, like the river before me.

In these rice-growing nations, the spoils of war were once the laborers of neighboring lands, who would be resettled to farm for the victorious nation. Wars see-sawed back and forth for centuries, creating a blurred ethnicity across the region due to the forced migration of so many over time.

However, in modern days, when the Indochina war threatened to spill across the region, it became imperative to insist that no commonality existed between neighboring states. There could be no regional brotherhood when communism threatened to stretch across the land.

Still, the people living where I stood were of the same ethnicity as those on the other side of the river.

But the river was vast and deep.

I waited there on the bank. The water moved with a certain power, slowly lunging towards the sea. It mesmerized after a while. Water mysteriously going down the river, hiding giant fish and a mysterious river dragon, all flowing from far away in primordial China.

I was waiting for something. Waiting, hopeful and fearful, knowing my life was flying by in far-off places.

A few boats crisscrossed in the distance. I could hear boat motors screaming nearby, out of sight. It was all peaceful.

My mind settled and I gave up considering all that had happened for now. There was no time for hand-wringing or celebration. I had to go on.

A thundering sunset loomed in the distance behind me, and its colors lay across the river. It was something magnificent, maybe something I could only ever see here, and I was here because I wanted to be a part of it.

But I could only be a scrounging immigrant, frittering away my days, childless and forlorn, using people and myself, vaguely realizing I might regret all this someday. But still choosing this. Choosing to be here. Such were the things the ambitious man thinks while waiting.

A few tiny boats flitted in every direction on the river before me, and the current continued on without regard for the water bugs on its surface.

The little boats were low to the water and had huge engines attached to poles that ran down into the water where propellers turned.

Then, in the shimmering distance, one boat was slowly growing. With each minute, it became clear it was heading towards me. Moving deliberately.

The boat grew as it neared, ear-splittingly loud, and I could see Andrew, grinning from ear to ear, seated in the bow.

Soon the boat settled into a glide and the engine was silenced and the prow lurched up onto the mud bank.

The concerned-looking boatman, hand on the engine, studied us both.

Andrew was talking before he stepped onto the shore.

"Yes, heard about the POWs? Yeah, I heard about... man said he heard there was some news..." He stepped onto the shore and bounded up to me.

"Oh, good to be back," he said, smiling his good-natured smile of honest English teeth. "Did you hear about this pub over here? They serve Guinness there."

He started to walk off before I had even said a word.

"We agreed to meet here, remember?" I said.

"Ah," he said with an exaggerated start.

"Andrew," I said. "The... the thing."

I was back to whispering the word.

He wheeled back to the boat and pulled out a plastic bag—the ubiquitous ones that were heedlessly discarded here and that blew in little tornadoes across vacant lots.

Holding it high, a gleeful look came across his face.

"It's here," he said.

The boatman looked extremely worried.

You see, I had arranged for Andrew to bring the thing over the border, over the river, to me.

The foolishness and the greed of those searching for it, and perhaps their underestimation of me, had let it slip through their fingers.

I sat the bundle on the riverbank and began opening it.

It was waiting for someone, waiting for me, in a plastic container—the kind to keep vegetables fresh, in a plastic bag, wrapped in tissue.

I lifted it out cautiously. A thin silver diadem, just like in the photos, sharp, elegant lines, and the pale blue gem. It was a stunning, unique, unclassifiable thing, light in my hands.

There were sweaty fingerprints staining it and I gently rubbed them off. They were mine.

Not long ago, I had thought that I was being tricked by everyone—Colm, Lori, Johnny, Maurice. I imagined the treachery against me behind the scenes. But I now realized that—I was the treacherous one. I had tricked them all. It made me feel both triumphant and sad.

I realized that both Andrew and the boatman were peering at it, as was I, their heads close to mine. I could smell the cheap morning whiskey already on both of their breaths. After a moment, it made me want to have a drink as well.

The boatman leaned away, looked at us both and shrugged his shoulders. It clearly meant nothing to him, but maybe he was relieved, thinking Andrew was having him ferry some contraband, maybe drugs, across the river, to another country.

As the boatman wheeled away to his never-ending crossing of the river, Andrew must have noticed me looking over to the far bank, back to that country.

"Someone over there?" he said.

"Yeah," I said.

"Why did you leave then?"

"I had to leave. I always have to leave."

There were other ways this could have worked out or maybe just this one. I had made my choice.

I stayed the night at a little guest house. Andrew and I had whiskey with the owner, a part-time fisherman who worked the river and skirted the nations, going back and forth over the river as the winds of commerce dictated.

He told us about when he used to catch giant fish in the river—colossal catfish, fished out semi-legally by teams of men, struggling in the mud of the river. The fish were now rare and never as big as they used to be. He assured us they would one day be gone for good. We drank a toast to the fish and its river. We had found the right place in the world.

The next morning, I found Andrew and said goodbye. He smiled his tired smile. The guest house owner was telling him tales of Western POWs hiding in the mountains which Andrew took for clues in his own quest.

On my way back to Bangkok, due to my finances, I had to take the slow, cheap local bus instead of the air-con one, much to the consternation of the bus driver, who, tried to persuade me that foreigners were not allowed on the local buses.

I insisted and we finally departed, but I soon saw his reason for not wanting me on the bus. There were trucks carrying illegally felled wood down this remote road. Maybe the wood was from another country; I didn't know. The air-con bus—which foreigners were supposed to take— left two times a day and all the illegal activity was off the roads then. Apparently, the locals could see this, but delicate foreigners like me were to be kept on the air-con buses.

The local bus stopped at a checkpoint mid-afternoon. Police boarded it and the driver immediately started telling them that a foreigner was on the bus and saying he was not to blame.

I did not want to be questioned or searched. I picked up a crumpled beer can from the floor and sat it on the seat next to me and pretended to be asleep. The idea was that it would be assumed I was drunk. This was ages ago when people more or less drank wherever and whenever they wanted in Thailand. Homemade whiskeys were sold by the ladleful everywhere. It was a paradise for the foreign drunk. It seemed that many of the Westerners coming here had, besides women, one thing on their minds—to be drunk constantly.

Thus, it was not a stretch for the police to believe I was drunk. And the thing was in the overhead compartment. How foolish to have come this far and then be caught out on some routine search.

The officer was not the confrontational type and only half-heartedly tried to wake me. I mumbled with closed eyes and put a sour expression on my face. I pulled my passport out of my pocket. All the proper entry stamps were there. The bus was free to continue.

Oh, drunkenness, how we forgive it and smile at its foolishness.

They had thought I was another hippie tourist, one from Europe who was unaccountably rich despite traveling on the cheap. The kind the nation wanted, until years later when they threw in the towel on the "high value" tourist model and encouraged the new ultra-budget tourist class of China to arrive. But then, I was still assumed to be a drunken tourist of value. And I escaped one last time.

The bus eventually dropped me back at the far western edge of Bangkok at a bus depot.

I made it back to my plain little room, the weekend behind me.

No matter how far I went, there was no escaping my dreams and no escaping my nightmares. And most of the time I wouldn't want to.

That night, I slept deeply while still awakening often and experiencing strange sounds and half memories.

31

The sidewalk was lined with vendors serving homemade confections, coconut juice, and mounds of fresh pineapple.

People complained about these vendors on footpaths, which made walking an obstacle course, as every sidewalk became a makeshift market.

The city authorities would go district by district, fining them. But they always came back.

Like the Thais, I enjoyed their convenience when I desired to buy some food but became annoyed at them for blocking the footpaths when I did not need something.

This street I was walking down was a street of embassies—mansions on green lawns and blocky fortresses with lines of Thais waiting for their visas. The road was filled with too many cars going to too many places—all of us on our way to someplace important.

On a future day, after terrorism outrages forced authorities to take security seriously around the world, the police would permanently clear this particular street of vendors, but today it was still a vibrant marketplace.

I passed by the vendors and the lines of visa supplicants, as I held the thing close to my chest.

Then I was in front of my destination.

It was the colossal U.S. Embassy in Bangkok, a true fortress, a modern castle, made necessary by low-tech car bombs.

These exotic structures were out of keeping with the local architecture. They were touted as denoting democracy and openness, but in their colossal scale and alien nature, said, "We are big, and you are small," not only to the locals (or "foreigners" as the embassy people might call them), but to me as well. Probably not a bad message to broadcast in these ethicless states.

I was interested in seeing the inside of the embassy, because regular U.S. citizens only ever got to step within the consulate, which was on the other side of the road—always much meeker architecture reserved for the sweaty U.S. countrymen renewing their passports and registering the foreign births of their children with the local ladies.

I showed my passport at the gate. A person, behind 3-inch-thick glass, popped her head up when she found my name on the list.

Passing through the gate, I stepped beneath the golden seal of the United States and its fierce eagle.

A young local man, who looked uncomfortable in a Western suit, showed me to a space-age meeting room.

It had a long white table under a swirling circular inset ceiling. White and shiny, it was an alien interior designed to awe. It had a Kubrickian aspect: white walls, floor and ceiling, broad and wide with unnervingly even lighting.

It was a studious attempt to show this place was from another land and made by another species. I imagined this was meant to provide the locals with a taste of the space-age land that made the rest of the world dance to its tune.

I did not have to wait. Indeed, they were waiting for me. If you have ever dealt with the overseas officialdom of your own country, you will know how rare that is.

Four Westerners stood at the sleek table—all expectant, as if waiting to judge me.

I was almost not surprised to find that Lori was one of them. She gave me a knowing smile of satisfaction.

The men were dressed in impractical Western blue business suits—the kind that required crisp, unrelenting air-conditioning.

Lori was wearing a short blue dress, insistent and alluring in its office chic, while just satisfying a sense of decorum.

She was now sneering at me, a lowly teacher in Bangkok, who was permitted to enter this glorious billion-dollar fortress of the age's Roman Empire.

I faced them in my polo shirt, rumpled and soaked to the skin from walking down the morning Bangkok street.

The men looked to Lori. She was in charge and thus would be the one to speak. She looked at me impatiently, head cocked.

"Okay, Mars. Let's see it," she barked in that way she had.

I knew then that she was impressed. I had shown her up after all. Shown them all up.

A black jeweler's pad was sitting on the white table. I carefully unpacked the parcel I had brought. I drew out the crown and set it on the black velvet. The Moon Gemstone shimmered a pale blue in the even white light of the room, almost in protest at its exposure to these foreign peasants.

I saw their reaction. They were awed.

No matter what bad things were fated to happen in the future, what dreams were to go unfulfilled, I would have accomplished this, at least this—another thing I cannot reveal to others. That would have to be enough.

One of the men, apparently a jeweler, probably brought into this meeting for this purpose, leaned forward, shaking a bit. He had a loupe in his hand but did not use it.

He lifted the crown and peered at it, turning it around to examine every part. After a moment, he turned to the others, about to speak, but could only nod his head.

All of us were transfixed, beholding it, a thing that had found its way after all this time into this foreign fortress.

Then the spell was broken, we all breathed again, and another man quickly covered the crown with a black, velvety fabric, as if to protect its virtue.

"You have luck," Lori said. "In more ways than you can imagine."

I looked down at the black fabric on the table and then back to her.

"You arranged things so that I would find Colm," I said. "But I found the crown too. That was lucky. But you knew it wasn't in the pot when you came to my room. You knew. Otherwise, you would not have been there with the others."

"I was pretty sure," she said. "It was important that everyone was of a feeling that it had not been found. Maintain the status quo."

"You are quite a diplomat," I replied.

She looked at me with pride. She had accomplished what she had set out to do.

"I'll take great pleasure in taking all the credit for this," she said and then laughed. "I'm joking. You'll have your reward."

"What I deserve, I guess." I laughed too. "Freedom waits for another day."

"It's a small country," she said. "Forever caught between big powers."

"Aren't we all?" I said.

"You saw the place," she continued. "Whatever the government, it's really no difference. It's just that with the government now, Americans can't set up businesses. Well, not easily. Not directly."

"It comes down to business?" I said sarcastically.

"You brought this to us for a reward, didn't you?" she said. "By your hand. Your cleverness. It would only disappear there. It is safe now until the day it is needed. And, uh, you know you better not go back there again. You were lucky to get out."

For a moment, I was lost in thought.

"I told you that you were the right person," she said. She said it like she had not believed it until this moment.

So, the thing was theirs. I trusted that my government would do the right thing. Giving it to them was the only thing to do. I wasn't going to melt it down or try to sell it on the black market. I wasn't sharp enough to do something that devious and fraught. I was only sharp enough to deal it to the U.S. government. They had sent a woman to get me to get it, and I had. Lori, no, my government itself, was my femme fatale.

I forgot to ask her about Colm, and had not heard from him since I returned, but I did not care anymore.

They had a reward for me—not money as I had demanded, but a job at a local U.S.-owned analysis company.

It paid well, and, I guess, gave the embassy plausible deniability that I was not being paid off for anything.

At first, I was annoyed, as I was not being directly paid for the crown, but the job afforded me experience and connections to people who knew what was going on. It was enough to feel that I had beaten Colm.

It also meant I did not have to go back to work teaching at the tutoring school. I walked away from the school. Never went back.

Sue back at the school would have said to me, "You're back?" in that way she almost smirked things rather than saying them. And Andrew would have expected me to come crawling back to my job there like I had done before. But not this time.

Andrew had walked away and was somewhere out there, liberating imaginary POWs. And Colm had got away with my money. But I had outsmarted them all. If I had gone back to the school, I would have been returning to a captivity of my own making. This was about going ever onward and that was what I would do. I was made for this.

I was developing a dread fear about going back—back to an old job, or back to a place I had lived before. I thought this was an admirable trait, but I wasn't entirely sure.

Working at the analysis company was enjoyable and something I was good at. It was a clipping service job, collecting local news items of interest to foreign clients—

news of drug patent infringement, possible border disputes, transnational crimes.

I never heard of the crown again, but knew it was out there somewhere, safe in the talons of the U.S. government.

I was Bert Mars, the man of providential fate, one who sometimes finds what he is looking for. I told myself I was doing the right thing by allowing the crown to be hidden away to wait for the right time to be revealed and not falling into hostile hands. And yet I knew some of the people involved and sympathized with them. I had seen the men working on the hills. I had walked through their mysterious night and heard its sounds.

I had put their crown into the maw of the Roman Empire of its day, which made its decisions for obscure reasons while telling me it was for the best. Maybe it was. It's a pragmatic world. And yet, I had taken it from them, from her, gaining something in return. It was hard to be a hero in the real world.

Eventually, I confided with a co-worker at the analysis company about the strange events of finding the crown. He surmised that the companies that built the hydroelectric projects in that country would have reason to want the status quo maintained so that their contracts would be upheld. The U.S. government would attempt to facilitate that.

Whether or not the finding of the crown would have made a difference, they would play it safe and make sure it did not end up causing any trouble.

So, my government was protecting businesses—and not even U.S. businesses. Those hydro projects were run by French companies. These were deals and considerations between developed nations—businesses that transcend and warp their own nations, involving things I could not begin to guess at.

For the long-suffering people, it was their fault they were in an inconsequential country, where big business and energy generation was profitable. It did not matter what kind of government they had, really. Business had to be made safe. It was always a web of Western interests two steps away from my grasp.

There would be no revolution. Multi-party politics for the young men farming on the sides of red hills was a luxury of far-off lands.

As I walked away that day, minus one mystical crown, it was hard to know whether I was playing chess, or I was just one of the pieces.

And in that, was I the one who had really thwarted a revolution? This question came to me sometimes. It came to me when I went to work and saw all the passive people on the bus, lost in their dreams in this capitalist paradise.

I knew I had taken it from her and had looked in her face denying it, but it was too late by then. As I sat at my new job at the analysis company, scheming and explaining the local foolish government to my foreign masters, I thought of this. And I thought it lucky no one knew all of my story. It was safely in my head, my rationalization machine forever trying to make me the innocent hero and everyone else a selfish villain.

I had done it. I had gotten to the bottom of it and out-maneuvered them all. Like I always intended to. I think this was the way things should have turned out, but I would never know.

I had collected the crown and put it in a drawer like the Keeper.

I had wanted my money back. And maybe I hadn't always been thinking straight. There are always regrets.

32

I never did get a school going. And I forgot about Matthew, our other partner on the school project, never finding him and updating him on what had happened. I only remembered him, quiet Matthew, months later, and then I felt embarrassed at my carelessness.

Andrew was lost somewhere at the border, doing his thing, searching for POWs.

It was a paradise we had found here. And it was a place to live and die, since we had to live and die.

"It'll be fine," as Colm would have said.

After a while, I saved enough money from my new job to get the lease on the beach land. I hadn't given up. I had learned that everything takes a long time, longer than I could ever imagine. It gave the chance for most people to give up.

The place I leased could not be registered as a hotel, as it had too few units—all of the places around there were like that, the tycoons who made up parliament wished it that way for some reason. Apparently, this was better for me because a properly registered hotel attracted taxes and scrutiny.

Soon after I took possession of the site, a nearby landlord started regularly burning tires in the next lot. I learned that he had wanted the lease for the land that I had and now he was trying to force me out.

I reported the burning to the police, but they laughed at me. The next day, the police made a show of openly talking to the man as he burned tires across from my place—showing me they were on his side.

Like many foreigners, I was dazzled by the realization that the country that I loved did not love me back. In fact, it was contemptuous of me. I existed only to enrich it.

Luckily, its sloppy incompetence ensured I ultimately got a lot more out of it than it did of me.

I guess that's at the heart of the bargain constantly being struck between my people and the rest. Each hopeful and each taking a chance. I smiled considering it all.

Soon, I was getting lots of inspections for proper documents at my beach land, no doubt part of the attempt to force me out. There were ways around all this. Officials would cooperate, and you had to pay. It was normal.

I traveled back and forth many times from Bangkok, getting things going at the beach land—the company structure, the proper electricity box, the rules for the zoning of the land, etc.

I was sure I would figure it out.

An old woman who ran a food cart on the street near my land told me that a girl had once drowned on the beach in front of my place. That's why all this was happening. That's why it was hard to get the place licensed and going. The beach was haunted and unlucky.

When I looked into the tangle of foliage near the beach, I expected to see the old caretaker, eyes peering out at me, thinking that I was the right person. He must be in a camp now, being educated by the state, which knew better.

Maybe it was the universe stopping me again. Yes, it was always hard to move above one's station.

Maybe I was becoming a collector of experiences. Someone who could not really know anything, as Deuan had thought. Yet still audacious, as Maurice would say.

I stood each evening at the beach. It was the time when the sun disappeared behind the mountains that separated the nation from Myanmar. The beach was plunged into cool shadow. For a time, it would be comfortable until the mosquitoes appeared, as if ordered to do so, driving me inside.

I was hopeful. That's all I could be. There was nothing to do but try and then keep trying. No one cared if I was a victim; neither did they care if I won. It was a man's slice of the world. I was small, but the big world was all mine.

There could never have been a revolution in any case. It was only the wishful thinking of the oppressed. And what I had done was the only thing to do.

Deuan had said I had taken it from them. Deuan, who was, no doubt, finding her way as the world worked against her.

I was sorry it had ended this way. We were each a tiny consciousness that happened to be together for a time. No need to be so sentimental. It was all done now.

There was something about being there, standing on the beach—it was hard to feel anything very deep and depressing. I stood there wearing my blood-red amulet, my acquiescence to superstition maybe, and I could only feel hopeful about tomorrow, about the future.

You can imagine what it was like, I'm sure—the pulsating waves, the continual wind, the vastness of the sea and sky, and then a sudden deep intake of breath that tells you it is working, that there is some peace here that the body can feel, even if the mind tries to keep going.

I was unsatisfied with my ambition sometimes. Was there more, some magic I was missing as an ambitious young man?

I would continue to fight. I guess most people fought hard, maybe because we were all alone, after all. I know some people aren't, but I was.

You can't have what you want. Not usually. Not really.

And here I was, smelling burning tires. I was getting used to it. That industrial smell, proving something man had made, trying to dislodge me, intimidate me in my paradise. They didn't know how strong and calloused a young man can become under pressure.

I was here at the beach. Not paradise, but harshness—sunburn, biting bugs, and regulations.

I was finally making my business in this strange world. I couldn't judge it. I couldn't complain. My problems were other's dreams.

I had fought my way here. It's always as hard as it can possibly be, so I'll just laugh. There's no other way.

The moon hung there that evening, immediate and out of reach, familiar and unknowable. It hung here over this paradise full of my problems, as I smelled burning tires. My life was getting full of stories now.

The winds came, a dusty torrent, and then the rain, thunderless, but pounding down in big drops. And the spell was broken. It was tropical rain. Rain you have to shut the windows for. Rain that's good to sleep by. The drains would handle the rain, sending it back to where it came. I would have to wait for a future day for the end to come.

For a time, it was still a struggle between my ambition and the salve of alcohol. Maybe they went together. Ambition burned me up and alcohol cooled me down. But I could still peer outside of myself and fear that I was ruining myself. I was not too far gone to know this.

I couldn't let my own ambitions and my own delusions burn me up anymore. Especially now that I was almost succeeding.

One day I stopped drinking so much and then another day I stopped entirely.

I don't know why, but things were finally looking up. I could feel it.

**** **** ****

Bert Mars returns in a NEW ADVENTURE in *Land Under Fallen Heaven*

The Bert Mars Adventures

Bert Mars, disillusioned by the promises of the world, pursues his fortunes in compelling and unforgiving Southeast Asia.

Book 1

In a Country with No Name

Bert Mars takes a chance and joins a coalition of shadowy interests to overthrow a government that has fallen afoul of the rich and powerful.

Based on true events, *In a Country with No Name* both horrifies and charms in its detailed account of an ambitious and desperate scheme.

Book 2

Edge of the Golden Moon

A fabled symbol of power... A long weekend... Stolen money... Too much alcohol...

While trying to recover his embezzled money, Bert Mars stumbles upon a hunt for an artifact that threatens revolution.

Bert is brought to the brink of ruin and revelation in a land where loyalties are only clear after it is too late.

Book 3

Land Under Fallen Heaven (Coming Soon)

Bert Mars unleashes international intrigue when he becomes embroiled in a scheme which is a cover for something truly sinister.

Faced with unimaginable stakes, his dreams and his honor are challenged.

Old friends and new unite in a chaotic unleashing of ambition and naiveté in a corrupt world.

RON MORRIS is a writer, political analyst, and traveler.

Books by Ron Morris

Land Under Fallen Heaven

Edge of the Golden Moon

Matter of a Thing Absolute

In a Country with No Name

There Are Still Unknown Places

Last Century

The Thai Book: A Field Guide to Thai Political Motivations

www.ingramcontent.com/pod-product-compliance
Lightning Source LLC
Chambersburg PA
CBHW030902060726
47591CB00005B/1385